Sherri

SpringSong & Books

Anne

Carrie

Cynthia

Jenny

Kara

Lisa

Michelle

Paige

Sherri

Sherri

Leila Prince Golding

BETHANY HOUSE PUBLISHERS
MINNEAPOLIS, MINNESOTA 55438

Sherri
Leila Prince Golding

Scripture quotation is taken from the HOLY BIBLE, NEW
INTERNATIONAL VERSION®. Copyright © 1973,
1978, 1984 by International Bible Society. Used by
permission of Zondervan Publishing House. All rights
reserved. The "NIV" and "New International Version"
trademarks are registered in the United States Patent and
Trademark Office by International Bible Society. Use of
either trademark requires the permission of International
Bible Society.

Library of Congress Catalog Card Number 85–71472

ISBN 1–55661–586–8
SpringSong Edition 1995
Copyright © 1985
Leila Prince Golding

Published by Bethany House Publishers
A Ministry of Bethany Fellowship, Inc.
11300 Hampshire Avenue South
Minneapolis, Minnesota 55438

Printed in the United States of America

To the memory of my mother,

whose prayers cover the beginning of this book.

1

*T*he small red Mustang handled well on the smooth pavement that curved in long rises and dips through the lush, green Indiana hill country. Going into a sudden steep climb between stands of pine and maple, Sherri McElroy was glad she had taken time to have the car thoroughly checked before starting out on this trip.

I hope this isn't some sort of wild goose chase, she thought. *But if it is, it's certainly an intriguing one.*

"And probably impossible, too," she said half-aloud as she fingered the short, heavy key hanging from a slim chain around her neck.

Then, a nagging feeling of foreboding coming over her, she impulsively slipped the key inside the neck of her gray wool sweater before putting her hand back on the steering wheel.

The key, along with the old gold watch in its leather pouch in her purse, was her reason for making this detour to a place she had never heard of a week ago, all to satisfy a dying patient's last request.

Her last case, as a private duty nurse for the elderly Joshua Fairbanks, had been routine at the beginning. She had started caring for Mr. Fairbanks in late February. Since he seemed to have no relatives, the hospital, following the direction of his lawyer, had transferred him from their intensive care unit to an apartment he owned in New York.

The stroke had left him paralyzed, but during the times

7

he was awake, his eyes followed Sherri's every movement. Often they would open suddenly from a time of prolonged sleep to gaze intently at her. Those deep-set gray eyes were clear, unmarred by the dullness that the combination of his age and a stroke could sometimes produce.

Sherri marveled at the intelligence and humor that seemed to be speaking to her from beneath his shaggy white brows. And because he seemed to want to communicate, she talked to him matter-of-factly, determined to encourage his apparent will to improve.

As she fed him and tended to his other needs, she told him about the day's weather or her views on news happenings they'd heard on the morning broadcasts.

During the late afternoons, she dug through the newspaper for sports scores, or interesting little human interest stories she thought might amuse him, and she was always rewarded for her effort with an answering twinkle from his eyes and the semblance of a smile on his twisted lips.

But it was evenings he seemed to enjoy most when, after she had prepared him for his night's rest, she read to him from the Bible. She had found it open on the bedside table the day she arrived to begin caring for him. When she started to remove it to make room for his first supper tray, she noticed the pleading look in his eyes.

Reading the Scriptures always seemed to quiet him, and for Sherri it brought back memories of her grandfather, sitting in the lamplight at twilight reading his copy of this book to her. Spiritual growth had seemed so important to her then, but things had changed, especially since her parents' death six years ago. Bible reading to Mr. Fairbanks created the first stirrings she'd felt in a long time of thoughts of God.

It was an evening about a month after she'd first come when, as she finished reading and closed the Bible, she heard a laborious, but discernible, "Ah-men."

Although the rest of his body remained as immobile as before, Mr. Fairbanks' ability to speak progressed well during the next few days. He engaged her in halting conversation as often as he could, and seemed to want to answer her questions about his life and his family. His wife had died years before, he told her, and though he had a son, they had had no contact for nearly twenty-eight years. "It was my fault," the old man admitted with tears in his eyes. "We had a sharp disagreement, and he left home before I had an opportunity to make things right."

"You never heard from him again?" Sherri asked, sympathy for his pain evident in her look.

"No," Mr. Fairbanks answered slowly. "There was a letter once, a couple of years later, a letter in unfamiliar handwriting. It said my son had married, and that they had a child, a son he named for me. But there was nothing else, no return address, and the postmark had been obliterated by rain. I had no way of responding."

His words had come with great difficulty, and Sherri remembered the sadness in his voice.

But not all their conversations centered around him. Mr. Fairbanks was quick to question Sherri about herself, and his interest in her answers seemed genuine. He would even tease her about the jottings she sometimes did in the little notebook she carried in the pocket of her uniform.

"This?" she laughed lightly. "Nothing profound. Just my thoughts and feelings."

Now, as Sherri deftly guided the little car, she thought about how that little notebook had been the basis of her first real talk with Joshua Fairbanks, one that later led to the strange request that followed.

Early one afternoon, waking from a nap, he had watched her writing in the book, lost in thought.

"Read some of that to me, Miss McElroy," he asked.

Then, as she hesitated, he said reassuringly, "I very much want you to."

"I really hadn't expected anyone but me to see this, Mr. Fairbanks. These bits of verse are just my thoughts."

"But we're friends, aren't we, you and I?" he pressed.

"All right," she said and began slowly turning the pages, stopping now and then to read a portion aloud.

> I ask you, God,
> Why do the good ones die?
> Why not instead the others,
> The ones who cheat and lie?
> Today, it's the roses,
> The first blooms opened at noon.
> Their beauty and perfume engulf me,
> Yet they, too, are gone . . . so soon.
> Yesterday I saw a child;
> Oh, not just any child, this one;
> One moment a laughing youngster,
> The next, someone's dying son.

Sherri stopped reading, and glanced at Mr. Fairbanks. He nodded for her to continue, so she turned a few more pages, then read,

> Of what do I secretly dream, you ask?
> I'll tell you—a beautiful home,
> A perfect loving family, but
> Mostly, to be never really alone.

Sherri sat silently a moment, her eyes on the page before her, wondering again about what mattered most in life. Then feeling his eyes on her, she read aloud,

> The stars tonight, do you see them?
> Their glory made me aware
> That perhaps it is true after all
> As I've been told; God does care.

"Thank you," Mr. Fairbanks said as she slipped the book back into her uniform pocket. "You are a fine young lady."

Then he smiled as best he could. "And your poem was right. God does care. He is concerned about the things that bother you and cause you grief. He cares, too, about your dreams and deepest desires."

"But if that's so," Sherri returned, "why does it always seem as though the world is just muddling along by itself? Oh, I know God showed His love by sending Jesus to die for us, but I can't understand how He permits things to happen as they do. There seems to be no reason at all to who lives and who dies, who is rich and who starves. It doesn't make any sense most of the time." As Sherri spoke, her tone changed from frustration to one tinged with bitterness.

"Oh, my dear," Mr. Fairbanks heaved a sigh, "your questions are sincere, I know. But throughout my long life, I've learned that God will make everything that happens in our lives turn out for our good if we permit Him to do as He chooses."

Sherri knew this kindly man had no intention of sermonizing, but his words made her uncomfortable, so she changed the subject.

"Thank you for listening to my little poems." She smiled at him. "I hope my grandfather appreciates them as well. I'll share some of them with him when I visit him next week."

"You're leaving?" The elderly man looked dismayed.

"Oh, just for a couple of weeks," Sherri reassured him. "I'm taking my vacation a bit early this year, and I'm driving to my grandparents' home in eastern Indiana. But don't you worry," she reassured him as she rose to adjust his sheets, and then draw the window shade against the afternoon sun. "The hospital will be sending out another nurse to care for you. And if you're lucky, you'll get one that chatters less than I do, so you can get some rest!"

"You spoke about your plans to drive to your grand-parents' home. My home in Indiana would not be much out of your way. Would you consider going there and delivering a most important message?"

She hesitated for just a moment, but then her heart went out to this old gentleman who had been so kind to her. "I'd be glad to," she said warmly. "Tell me about the mes-sage."

"It's for my grandson, Joshua. He's arriving in town, and I won't be there to meet him. I want you to find him, and give him some things I came here to New York to collect for him."

Sherri looked at him, confused. "Your grandson? But Mr. Fairbanks, I thought you didn't know the boy's where-abouts. Or your son's either."

"I didn't, until about two months ago. Then he wrote me. He said his mother had died, and he'd found my ad-dress in her things. He seemed to want to meet me as much as I wanted to meet and be with him. He sounds like a young man I'd be proud to call my grandson. His coming to Scar-borough is a fulfillment of my life's dream."

Mr. Fairbanks looked away for a moment, then cleared his throat before continuing. "I came here to New York to get some things I want him to have, but then I got sick . . ." His voice trailed off.

"Mr. Fairbanks?" Sherri asked, concerned.

"I'm all right. I don't want him to arrive with no one to meet him, and no one to let him know how much it means to me that we will finally be together."

"I can understand that," Sherri said, pulling out her lit-tle notebook. "Now, sir, if you'll give me the directions to your home?"

He dictated slowly as she took them down. As he finished, she closed the book. "You said there was something you wanted me to give him."

"Oh, yes. You'll find a letter for Joshua in my desk drawer in the house. It may take a bit of fiddling under the drawer to locate it, but a bright girl like you shouldn't have any trouble." He smiled affectionately at her.

"Then in the top drawer of the bureau over there, you'll find the watch."

Sherri rose, laid aside her notebook, and slid the bureau drawer open.

"Way in the back, on the right side behind the shirts," he continued. "It's in a leather pouch."

"This must be it." Sherri returned to the bed and laid the small brown packet on the coverlet near his arm, loosening the tie.

She drew out a man's gold pocketwatch. The gold felt cool and heavy in her hand, and she could tell it was very old.

"It belonged to my grandfather," Mr. Fairbanks said, "a gift from his wife."

"It's lovely!" Sherri exclaimed as she turned it over, finding that the back and front were both engraved alike in a pattern of winding roses encircling a pair of doves.

When she pushed a small projection opposite the winding-stem, the cover opened, revealing the face of the timepiece. Inside the cover, there appeared to be an inscription, but before Sherri could try to make it out, Mr. Fairbanks brought her attention back to the leather pouch.

"There's a very special key in there, too," he told her.

Sherri turned the pouch upside down, and a tarnished brass key fell out. "It's so heavy for its size, and so ornate. These are lovely gifts for your grandson," she smiled at the elderly man. "I'm sure that with these, and your letter, too, he'll know how welcome he is."

Mr. Fairbanks sighed, suddenly looking very tired. "I

seem to be feeling quite drained," he said slowly. "Perhaps it's time that I sleep. I'll have the nurse who comes tomorrow contact my housekeeper in Scarborough to let her know you are coming and to prepare for you. You'll find the keys to my house over there in my wallet. Please take them."

He paused and closed his eyes a moment, and Sherri wondered if he had gone to sleep. But then he opened them slowly.

"I've enjoyed knowing you, Miss McElroy," he said gently. "I know that God will enable you to handle anything in life if you'll just let Him."

"Why, Mr. Fairbanks," she said, taking his hand, "you sound as if we're saying goodbye forever. I'll be gone only a couple of weeks; then I'll be right here with you again. But I'll miss you while I'm gone. I really will." She leaned over and kissed him lightly on the forehead, then pulled a cover up over him. He closed his eyes again, this time relaxing into sleep.

He had known more than she about their next meeting. The following afternoon, as she was closing her last suitcase in preparation to leave for the drive to Indiana, a call came from the hospital. Mr. Fairbanks had just suffered a massive heart attack and died.

2

Sherri's thoughts snapped back to the present. Her foot left the gas pedal and began tapping the brake.

Red flags and signs warned of a work project around the upcoming sharp curve. Moving cautiously ahead, she was waved toward a cutoff by a hard-hatted construction worker.

"Oh, drat," she said aloud, hoping she wouldn't be taken far off her route. However, as the miles bumped past, the blacktop road led to a gravel one that degenerated into a rutted dirt lane, and she began to get exasperated.

Her exasperation had turned to concern before a sign finally directed her back to the highway. She supposed it had been the most direct route possible for a detour in the hilly, rural area, but it had wasted so much time.

She glanced worriedly at the few streaks of color remaining low on the horizon from the setting sun. The sky seemed to be darkening quicker than it should have for so early in the evening. She depressed the gas pedal until the speedometer registered the limit posted along the highway.

Sherri's concern grew as she noticed a few small dark clouds moving slowly across the sky as the daylight faded. Driving in a storm was not her idea of fun.

I'd hoped to reach Scarborough long before now, she thought. *Maybe I can accomplish what I have to and get on my way even this evening.*

But on second thought, she knew it would be impossible. For after reaching the town, she had no idea how long it might take to locate Mr. Fairbanks' house. Besides, she noticed how tired she was beginning to get. She had spent an uncomfortable night in a noisy hotel and had started out very early that morning, stopping along the way only long enough for a sandwich and to refill the gas tank. Even if there was no storm, it might not be wise to go much farther without some rest.

Then she saw the sign, "Scarborough, 5 miles," and sighed with relief.

Entering the town, she saw on her left, outlined against the darkening sky, a high, pine-covered hill. Halfway down, its northern face was scarred by a long, jagged outcrop of rock she supposed gave the town its name.

"Now to find Elmhurst Road," Sherri muttered, checking the directions Mr. Fairbanks had given. But a check of what seemed to be the main streets turned up no such place. "No choice but to ask," she said aloud, and headed back for the small service station she had noticed at the first stop sign.

The young man who appeared at her car window seemed vaguely familiar. She wondered fleetingly whom he reminded her of.

"Check your oil?" His smile above the firm, angular chin was friendly but casual.

"Yes, will you please?" Sherri stepped from the car and moved to where he bent over the engine of her car. "Could you direct me to Elmhurst Road? I'm trying to locate the Fairbanks residence."

The man became very still, the dipstick poised. Then he straightened, wiping the stick with a rag, slowly, carefully as though it were a very delicate task. A light breeze lifted a lock of his brown hair and dropped it in a glossy curve over his forehead.

When he turned, a pair of deep-set gray eyes met hers.

"You'll have to take this highway out of town about three miles. Elmhurst Road angles off to the left just after you cross the bridge."

She started to say "thank you," but he continued talking as he finished the oil-check and closed the hood. "I don't think you'll find anyone home out there. I understand Mr. Fairbanks is out of town."

"Yes, I know," Sherri said, then checked herself, wondering if she should say any more.

He looked questioningly at her for a moment, then went to the rear of the car. As he replaced the gas cap, he asked, "Are you a relative of Mr. Fairbanks?"

"No, I'm just a friend." She paused briefly. "Sort of a business acquaintance. Sherri McElroy." Then she wished she'd not given her name.

"Oh, I see." Then he grinned, "I'm Josh Stevens. Be careful when you get on Elmwood. Looks like we might get some rain any minute, and I understand that particular stretch of blacktop gets a bit slippery when it's wet."

"All right, thank you."

After she had paid him and settled back behind the wheel, he pushed the door shut for her. "You may see Mrs. Morrow, the Fairbanks' housekeeper. She and her husband live on the grounds." He paused a moment, as if he wanted to say more, but another car had pulled in to the full-service pumps and the driver was in no mood to wait. "Hey! Hurry it up!" he yelled. So the young man turned to help him, flashing Sherri a warm grin as she drove away.

Midway through the little town, Sherri slowed her car at the small hotel-restaurant she had noticed earlier.

"I'm getting hungry," she said to herself. "It's been a long time since that sandwich at lunch, and I suppose I should check to see if a room is available. It's obvious I'm not going to get away from this town before dark."

Starting to pull into a parking space, she noticed how

unpromising the place looked and decided to go on.

"I really should have asked if there was a decent motel nearby," she said half aloud, wondering if she should go back to the gas station and inquire. But she discarded the notion and in a few minutes the town was behind her. Perhaps the housekeeper Josh Stevens might have mentioned might be able to suggest a more suitable place to stay. She had no intention of driving alone on a stormy night.

She had no difficulty finding the road she wanted; it was well marked. As she turned south onto Elmhurst Road, she switched on the headlights.

Shortly afterward, she found the drive that curved away from the road through an avenue of pines. Straight and tall, the trees rose in stately watchfulness on either side of the drive, moving slightly in the breeze that was beginning to blow. *They're beautiful,* Sherri thought as she guided the car effortlessly around what proved to be the last gentle bend before arriving at the residence.

At the sight of the house, Sherri gasped. "Why, it's a mansion!" she said. "I didn't expect to find anything like this."

Although darkness was settling over the landscape, she could see the outline of the large house at the top of a low, broad landscaped rise of ground. The sliver of moon appearing on the horizon, intermittently covered by gathering black clouds, briefly illuminated the house and grounds, giving her momentary glimpses of what seemed to be a large estate.

Sherri parked near the entrance, the headlights sweeping across terraced lawns and the tall white pillars of a veranda.

She picked up her purse and started to get out of the car. Then she reached for her overnight bag. "As long as there's obviously enough room," she murmured, "perhaps Mrs. Morrow won't mind if I ask to spend the night here.

It sure beats that dumpy hotel in town, and Mr. Fairbanks did say he'd instruct her to make me welcome."

She locked the car and stood looking at the immense white pillars reaching upward, the shuttered windows, the towering chimneys. But there seemed to be no lights anywhere, and the evening was darkening quickly.

Her gaze returned to an upper window that seemed to be partially raised, a bit of drapery or curtain blowing outward in the rising wind.

A jagged streak of lightning and sharp clap of thunder made her jump. She realized that bits of foliage were beginning to swirl across the drive and there was a sudden coolness in the air.

Sherri hurried up the flagstone walk between bushes swaying in the now strong breeze. Half running up the wide stone steps, she crossed the veranda. Her hand searched and fumbled for a doorbell she couldn't locate.

Another bright jag of lightning showed her a large brass knocker centered on the carved door. She lifted it and it fell with a heavy metallic thud. She waited. Perhaps Mrs. Morrow was off in another part of this huge house, and hadn't heard.

She knocked again and again.

There was no sound now but that of the strong wind rising in fury among the bushes and trees. Heavy drops of rain began to fall, tentatively, then quicker, harder, driven by the forceful gusts.

I don't believe this, Sherri thought.

Suddenly remembering the house keys Mr. Fairbanks had told her to take from his wallet, she fumbled in her purse and found them. Searching in the dimness for a keyhole, she finally inserted the larger of the two keys, discovering with relief that it turned easily. She pushed the door open and stepped into the darkness of the house.

Sherri felt along the wall until she found a light switch.

Flipping it, she turned to find herself in a large, ornate foyer. High above her, a crystal chandelier gave its light through glittering prisms. The white marble floor flowed toward gilt chairs and a large brass hall tree. Her quick glance took in the paintings on the opposite walls. Across the expanse from the door, a lovely wide staircase rose upward, flanked by balustrades of polished dark wood.

Sherri shook her head, amazed. Who would have guessed Mr. Fairbanks would own all this? His New York apartment had been simple enough. This grandson she was to meet was going to be in for some big surprises if he knew as little as she did about Mr. Fairbanks.

But now to find the housekeeper.

"Hello?" she called.

After a few moments' silence, she tried again, louder. "Hello? Anyone here? Mrs. Morrow?" Her calls were answered by stillness. Sherri felt uneasy and unsure about what to do.

Perhaps the housekeeper had gone for a few minutes. The man at the gas station said she and her husband had a home here on the property, and she certainly hadn't known the exact time to expect Sherri's arrival. The storm seemed to be worsening quickly now; perhaps Mrs. Morrow was waiting for a break in the rain before returning to the main house.

I don't blame her, Sherri thought. *This house is beautiful, but I don't think I'd want to stay here alone during a storm either.*

"Might as well explore a bit while I wait," Sherri told herself. "Looks like this is to be my home for the night, and there's certainly no tour guide." Perhaps it was just as well. She needed to find Mr. Fairbanks' letter, and this way no explanations to the housekeeper would be necessary. If she could find the letter now, she could deliver his legacy to the old gentleman's grandson in the morning, and be on her way.

She put her overnight bag down beside one of the cushioned chairs, being careful not to let the damp case brush against the heavy satin.

The first door on the left revealed a small, formal parlor. Sherri glanced around at the two Victorian love seats, a few carved-back velvet chairs. A tea table positioned in front of a small marble fireplace conjured up images of elegant entertaining.

She drew in her breath as she opened the next door. "Would I like to spend time here!" she said aloud. The light from the foyer did not brighten this room as well as it had the other one, but a flash of lightning through the tall windows had illuminated walls lined from floor to ceiling with shelves of books.

Unable to find a light switch, she turned on one of the lamps near a large, deep chair. Perhaps this was Mr. Fairbanks' study.

Several richly upholstered, high-backed chairs covered in soft leather were placed around the room with comfortable footstools drawn up before them. Lamps and small tables stood conveniently nearby. But as she glanced around, she saw that there was no desk, and that was what she had to locate.

Then Sherri noticed the long, narrow writing table placed beneath one of the ceiling-high mullioned windows. Could this be what she was looking for?

Pulling back the little carved chair from in front of the table, she slid open the drawer.

"No luck," she said aloud, looking down at the plain white paper and heavy square envelopes stacked neatly beside a row of pens and a bottle of ink. "Just a correspondence desk."

She started to close the drawer, then remembering

something Mr. Fairbanks had mumbled, she pulled the drawer all the way out and set it on the wide, gilt-edged blotter on top of the table.

Stooping down, she peered into the opening where the drawer had been, but saw nothing. Reaching her hand in, she groped around, but finding nothing, she replaced the drawer and turned away, disappointed.

"Perhaps I misunderstood what he was trying to tell me," she mused, "or maybe his mind was wandering. But he seemed so definite. Finding this letter may be tougher than I thought."

She returned to the foyer and crossed the marble floor. The wide double doors she had not yet explored opened into an especially large room with a floor of polished wood. She could just make out the gold and red brocade draperies covering the many windows that reached to the high frescoed ceiling.

The huge room was bare except for a grand piano and a number of gilt chairs lining the walls. She could barely see in the dimness a few more chairs that stood on a raised platform at one end of the room.

"Probably for musicians," she mused aloud, visualizing parties that may have been held there.

The next room proved to be a spacious formal dining room. The subdued sheen of fine, well-worn silver pieces gleamed from the large sideboards and buffets. Red velvet seats cushioned the chairs positioned around the long table.

Through an archway at the right end of the room, Sherri could see down a hallway to what might be a kitchen. A faint light glowed there, and she decided that perhaps Mrs. Morrow had returned at last.

"Hello," she called. Then louder, "Hello?"

But the kitchen was empty. The light she had seen was a small one near a chintz-curtained window. "It may be an automatic night light, since no one seems to be here," she decided.

This was beginning to get disturbing. Where *was* Mrs. Morrow anyway? Her employer had instructed her to be ready for a guest.

But Sherri's irritation softened when she flipped the light switch above the kitchen counter and spied a tray all set with a cheery yellow coffee service and plates. Beside them, a yellow-checkered cloth covered a large platter. Lifting the edge, Sherri took in the wonderful fragrance of fresh bread and coffee cake.

Preparations had been made for her arrival, after all. She chided herself for her harsh feelings toward the housekeeper. Mr. Fairbanks had been in his eighties; perhaps this Mrs. Morrow was elderly, too, and had already retired for the night. Or perhaps she was hard of hearing and didn't realize Sherri had arrived.

Sherri felt safer now. After all, the bread was still warm. Mrs. Morrow couldn't be too far away.

Actually there's no need to bother her tonight, Sherri thought. *I can leave her a note that I've decided to stay over, then find myself a place to sleep. She probably has guest rooms kept ready. But coffee and some of that fresh bread are going to be a must before bed.*

Sherri picked up the coffeepot and filled it at the sink, then measured out coffee from the cannister nearby. Carrying the pot to the stove, she set it over a low flame. While the coffee brewed, she could find a room and settle in.

Sherri picked up her purse and went into the foyer for her overnight case. She hadn't noticed any bedrooms in the areas she had checked, so she supposed they were upstairs and headed toward the staircase.

Along the wall where the bottom of the curved bannister flared outward stood a long, low table, its surface glowing softly with the mellowness of years of polishing. As she passed it, Sherri smoothed her hand along its edge, enjoying the beauty and sense of times past. *It must be very old*, she thought.

Gently she touched the pair of old-fashioned oil lamps that sat on the lace runner, their tall glass chimneys rising above ornate brass bases, and wondered if they were kept handy in case of electrical failure. *Glad I noticed them*, she thought, especially with the storm tonight, and Mrs. Morrow not in sight.

Mounting the curving staircase, her hand flowed over the smoothness of the wide balustrade.

At the top, in the half-dark, she groped unsuccessfully for a light switch. Peering through the gloom, she could dimly perceive a light fixture on the opposite wall. To her surprise, the sconce held candles instead of light bulbs. Candles? Could it be there was no electricity on the second floor?

She began to feel uneasy, then a bit frightened. She remembered the times when, as a child, she would throw the bedcovers over her head to hide from the nameless, invisible scary things that seem to inhabit the dark of a room when one is alone.

"Stop it," Sherri chided herself. "I thought you left those silly imaginings behind years ago."

This was, after all, a very old house, and Mr. Fairbanks had lived here alone. Perhaps his bedroom was downstairs, and he seldom used this second floor, so never installed lights here. Mr. Fairbanks showed an erratic streak of frugality. His New York apartment had been modest when he obviously could have afforded much more luxury. Besides, she had been without electricity before. She remembered evenings at her grandparents' farm when storms like this would knock down power lines, and the three of them would sit together around the flickering flame of the oil lamp. The oil lamp . . . of course! That's why they'd been placed on the table downstairs in the foyer.

Quicky she descended the stairway to the table where the lamps stood. Lifting the lid from a small covered brass urn, she found matches. She lighted the wick and replaced the glass chimney over the bright flame. After turning the little knob to adjust the flame and stop the fine wisp of smoke that was clouding the glass, she picked up the lamp and again started up the staircase.

The flickering light created weird, contorted shadows that accompanied her up the stairs, and childhood apprehensions began to steal over her again. At the top of the stairs, she stopped and listened intently. Did she hear a sound that was not the wind or the rain?

The long, carpeted hall stretched out into the darkness in front of her, lighted only by lightning flashes in the windows at the far ends, and the dim glow of her little lamp. She shivered, wanting to turn and run. Maybe sleeping up here wasn't such a good idea after all.

Then the familiar aroma of perking coffee reached her nostrils, and she laughed unsteadily at herself.

"Afraid of the dark, Sherri?" she said aloud. She was a bit afraid, of course, but she determined this big, lonely house would not get the best of her.

She crossed the hall to a door that seemed somehow familiar. It was of a mellow dark wood, its borders deeply carved with twining roses circling a pair of doves.

Adjusting her purse strap on her shoulder, and shoving her case ahead of her with her foot, she reached for the burnished knob.

Her vague sense of uneasiness began to mount to fear again, but biting her lip, she resolutely pushed the door open.

3

Sherri stepped through the doorway, the glow of the lamp preceding her. Its illumination revealed a spacious but intimate bedroom. At that moment her uneasiness subsided in her delight at the room before her.

The soft rich colors of a Persian rug covered most of the floor, and a four-poster bed with a filmy canopy and hangings dominated one corner of the room.

Carefully she set the lamp on a low table beneath a tall mirror. *How lovely,* she thought. A blue brocade chaise lounge was tucked in an alcove. Folded on it was a quilted, ivory satin throw next to several matching small pillows. "Staying here won't be so bad after all," she smiled.

Stepping out of her low-heeled pumps, she felt the marvelous softness of the rug beneath her feet. Through a partly opened door, she could see a complete but old-fashioned bathroom.

Hanging her jacket and purse in the tall empty wardrobe, she brought her overnight case in and, putting it beside the lamp, snapped it open. She took off her slacks and sweater, then slipped into a robe and slippers. "Now for some of that coffee," she said aloud.

Knowing this charming hideaway waited for her would make the climb up those darkened stairs easier next time. To help push away the dark shadows, she removed the chimney from a lamp sitting on a bedside table. Taking a match from a crystal container next to it, she held the flame to the wick. Pendants around the lamp's base glowed like rubies as she replaced the chimney. The room seemed warmer and cozier now, and Sherri relaxed a little as she headed for the kitchen.

The coffee smelled wonderful. Sherri turned off the burner, poured a cup for herself, and carried it to the round table in the center of the room. She pulled the chain of a hanging lamp positioned directly above the table, the light shining softly through stained glass and prisms.

Sherri let the coffee warm her, then reached for an apple from the bowl of fruit on the table.

Her hand stopped midway to the bowl. *What was that noise?* She listened intently, certain she had heard something this time. It was a different sound than before, but clearly discernible above the steady pounding of the rain. The sound seemed to come from somewhere out front. Sherri rose and headed through the hall and to the dining room.

When she reached the foyer, she was sure now that her ears weren't deceiving her. She had heard something over the storm. But what?

As she reached the door, she let out a sigh of relief. A car motor. Mrs. Morrow must have finally come. Thank goodness. Two hours alone in this house on a stormy night was quite enough.

With a smile of greeting, she opened the door. Her hand froze.

There was no Mrs. Morrow! Instead, a car with its lights off was moving slowly away from where her car was parked.

As the rain drummed heavily on the veranda steps, she saw the car slide like a shadow almost silently toward the drive's first curve. Then suddenly, as though the driver had seen the lighted doorway, the car speeded up and disappeared into the darkness of the storm.

With pounding heart, Sherri swiftly closed the door

and clicked the lock. Her other hand still gripped the knob as frightening thoughts crowded in. Had she locked the door behind her when she arrived? Had someone come in, or was someone in the house all the time? Why no lights on the car? Who was trying to get away without being seen?

The questions swirled in her mind, making her more frightened.

She turned and half ran back to the security of the kitchen and leaned against the counter. What should she do? Her first impulse was to get into her car and head for town, but what if whoever was in the car was waiting for her at the end of the drive? Surely her chances would be better here in the house than stranded in her car on that isolated stretch of highway she'd driven to get out here. And Josh Stevens had told her the blacktop was dangerous in the rain. What if she had an accident, and no one found her, or worse yet, what if the stranger in the car found her?

Sherri sank into a chair and leaned her head into her hands. She had to keep her wits about her and not panic. The police. She could call the police. Surely this little town had a sheriff. Her eyes searched the kitchen for a phone. None here? Perhaps in the hall . . . or the foyer. But as she started out of the kitchen, she caught herself.

If she talked to the police, what was she going to say? How was she going to explain her presence in the house? She was a stranger here, and had entered the house without anyone seeing her. If the stranger in the darkened car had stolen something, perhaps the police might blame her. No one here could verify her relationship to Mr. Fairbanks, no one but Mrs. Morrow.

Mrs. Morrow. Of course! She might still be in the house. The thought of her steadied Sherri, and she turned back to the kitchen. She had better find her, if she was to be found. Mrs. Morrow might have a simple explanation for the car.

"I'm going to feel pretty silly if all my fears prove groundless," Sherri told herself. "The car could have been just kids playing a prank, or maybe even someone dropping Mrs. Morrow off. I'm sure a house this size has multiple entrances, so she could have come in through another door."

But where to look for her? Sherri picked up her coffee cup as she considered the options. One thing was certain. Heading down that long, dark hall upstairs would be a last resort. Best to check the lighted areas first. And didn't servants usually stay on the first floor in houses like this so they could be near the kitchen?

"Mrs. Morrow?" she called, pushing the swinging door open slightly. "Mrs. Morrow?"

As she listened for a reply, she caught her breath. Coming from the front of the house, she heard a loud, insistent, repeated thudding. Sherri froze. Someone was pounding on the front door. Had the intruder come back for her?

She could try to find a back way out of the house, but then what? Her car was parked right in front of the entrance. Whoever was knocking stood less than twenty feet from it. What if the person in the car had an accomplice? Could someone be waiting at the back door for her? She'd have to find a place in the house to hide, a place where she could lock herself in, and hope they'd go away, or that someone . . . anyone . . . would come to help before it was too late.

She stood in the middle of the kitchen, clutching the table edge for support, trying to decide which way to go, when she heard a muffled voice calling her name. "Miss McElroy?" *Thud* . . . "Miss McElroy? Are you in there?" *Thud, thud.* "Sherri?"

He knew her name?

"Miss McElroy," the man's voice called, "if you're all right, please come to the door. I'm Josh Stevens from the gas station. I must speak to you."

It was just the man she'd met earlier, the one with the gray eyes and the friendly grin. Sherri felt a rush of relief, and pushing her hair back from her eyes, tried to regain some sense of composure as she hurried to unlock the door.

He stood there, his hair and jacket dripping from the rain. "Josh, what happened to you? Car trouble?"

He looked down at his soggy garb, and grinned at her. "Not exactly. Can I come in?"

"Oh, of course, I'm sorry," she said, stepping aside and opening the door wider. "It's just that I'm so surprised to see you here. Do you need to warm up? I have some coffee on."

"Sounds great," he said, pushing the dark hair away from his forehead. He took off his jacket and his muddy shoes and deposited them by the door, then followed her to the kitchen.

"Hey, this is nice," he whistled admiringly.

"It is beautiful, isn't it?" Sherri smiled at him. She decided against telling him that just a few hours before she'd been just as awestruck with the rich surroundings. *Although Josh knows of Mr. Fairbanks, he's apparently never been inside the house before tonight, but maybe not many others have, either.*

"Maybe I can find some towels for you," she said as she turned up the flame under the coffeepot. "The coffee will be warm in a minute."

A quick search through the cabinets turned up a stack of soft hand towels. Josh dried his thick hair and his face, then sponged off his clothes. "Thanks," he smiled at her. "I'm feeling warmer already."

The coffee was steaming as Sherri located a cup and saucer in the cabinet, filled a cup for Josh, and handed it to him. She joined him at the table, then lifted the checkered napkin from the bread tray to uncover the round, fragrant loaf.

"Homemade bread," Josh observed. "Is Mrs. Morrow to be credited for this, or have you been doing some quick baking since your arrival?"

"I can bake," Sherri laughed, "but I'm not that fast. Would you like some?"

He reached for the long, sharp bread knife on the tray as Sherri got up to pour herself some fresh coffee. When she turned from the stove to face him again, she realized he hadn't sliced into the bread. The friendly grin was gone from his face, and he fingered the blade of the long knife before he spoke to her.

"Are you alone here?" he asked.

Sherri felt a cold chill sweep over her as she looked at the knife. Why did he want to know if she was alone? Who was this man, anyway? In her relief at a familiar voice, she had let him in without thinking. But what did she know about him? He was the only one in this town who knew she was here.

She looked back at him, then down at the knife. In inviting him in, she may have just opened the door to danger.

4

Sherri felt sure Josh could see the sudden fear in her eyes.

"Sherri, did I say something wrong? All I wanted to know was whether or not you are alone. Did you find Mrs. Morrow?"

She cleared her throat, and leaned hard against the counter behind her. "No, no . . . nothing wrong. Mrs. Morrow . . . well, she's, I think she's in her room in the back now." It wasn't exactly a lie; she didn't know for sure where Mrs. Morrow was.

Josh studied her as she spoke, but chose to ignore her sudden nervousness, and leaned forward to cut himself a thick slice of bread from the loaf. He then laid the knife on the bread board, and leaned back in his chair.

Seizing her chance, Sherri grabbed the bread tray, knife and all, and moved it to the counter behind her. "I'll slice more," she explained in response to Josh's puzzled look. Now the knife was firmly in her possession. If anyone was going to wield a weapon, she wanted it to be her.

Sherri wasn't sure whether seconds or minutes were passing. She felt suspended in a vacuum of half-panic, wondering if she was truly in danger or was imagining it all.

Just then Josh stood and moved slowly toward her, his deep, gray eyes probing her. Sherri backed away toward the door, her hand feeling behind her back for the bread knife. She felt the blade, then the wooden handle, and clasped it tightly. But as she pulled it forward, the blade caught on the edge of the tray, and the knife flew out of her hand and clattered noisily onto the tile floor.

Josh looked down at the knife, then at Sherri as a look of understanding and compassion crossed his face. "Oh, Sherri, you've got it all wrong! I'm not here to hurt you. I only came out here tonight because I was afraid you might be stranded. My landlady, Martha Kirk, is a friend of Mrs. Morrow's. When I mentioned to her about your arrival here, she decided to call Mrs. Morrow to let her know you'd be coming. When she did, we discovered the phone lines must have been downed by the storm. I realized then if you'd had any trouble getting here, there would be no way you could call for help, so I came to be sure you were all right. That's all. That's the truth."

Why she believed him, Sherri wasn't sure. Something about the sincerity in those eyes made her believe his story was true. After the frights this house had held so far, she felt she had to trust someone.

"I believe you, Josh. What I said before about Mrs. Morrow? It wasn't exactly true. I'm not sure at all she's here. When you came to the door, I didn't know who it was. I was so afraid . . ." Her voice gave way and she looked down at the floor.

Josh moved toward her and grasped each of her arms in his strong hands. "Well, you are safe now," he reassured her. "And I can stay as long as you'd like."

He slipped one hand under her chin and tilted her head up toward his face so their eyes met. "Are you going to be all right?"

Sherri managed a little smile, and then looked down, embarrassed. "I am, yes."

"In that case, let's enjoy some of that homemade bread. And this time, you can do all the slicing. Okay?"

Sherri nodded, and they both laughed. He followed her

to the table and pulled out a chair for her. He retrieved the bread tray, and warmed their coffee before he settled himself at the table beside her.

"Sherri, how well do you know Joshua Fairbanks?"

Obviously Josh didn't know Mr. Fairbanks was dead. Perhaps word hadn't reached this small community yet. If it hadn't, perhaps Fairbanks' grandson wouldn't have heard yet, either, and it was only right that family be told first. She could still be honest with Josh without telling him everything.

She shrugged her slim shoulders as she looked up at Josh. "I don't know him well. You see, I'm a nurse in New York, and Mr. Fairbanks has been a patient of mine the last few weeks. When he found out I was coming in this direction on vacation, he asked me to stop at his home and make a delivery. That's all."

A look of consternation crossed Josh's face. "He's ill? What is wrong with him?"

Surprised by the deep urgency in his voice, Sherri paused. Josh seemed to really care about Mr. Fairbanks. Should she tell him about the old man's death? "He's been bedfast for a few weeks," Sherri answered carefully, "recovering from a stroke. Was . . . is he a friend of yours?"

Now it was Josh's turn to become silent. He looked down into his empty coffee cup, then up to study Sherri's face. Under his wide, straight thick brows, the gray of his eyes seemed to darken as they searched hers.

"Sherri, tonight I asked you to trust me." He paused for a moment. "Can I trust you?"

Sherri straightened. "Trust me? Of course you can trust me. But what . . ."

Josh held up a hand to silence her. "There's something I want to tell you, something no one else here knows. But I need to know you will keep it in confidence until my . . . until Mr. Fairbanks returns. Will you agree?"

Sherri looked at him for a moment, the seriousness of his face showing her that he wasn't playing games. "I promise, Josh."

"Joshua Fairbanks," he said slowly, "is my grandfather, though we've never met face-to-face. My father left home when he was young, and they never had contact with each other again, so I've never seen my grandfather. We've only recently found each other, and I came to Scarborough so I could finally meet him."

Sherri's mind raced as she tried to piece together what Josh was saying with the information Mr. Fairbanks had given her. This gas station attendant was Mr. Fairbanks' grandson?

"But your name isn't Fairbanks," Sherri reminded him.

"Oh, that," he chuckled sheepishly. "I am named after my grandfather, Joshua Stevens Fairbanks. But when I arrived here and found he was gone, I decided it might be wise to keep my identity a secret until we'd had a chance to meet, so I dropped the Fairbanks and became Josh Stevens."

Sherri was still confused. "You weren't supposed to arrive in town until tomorrow. And if you just came to Scarborough, what are you doing with a steady job?"

Now it was Josh's turn to look surprised. "How did you know I wasn't expected here until tomorrow?"

"Mr. Fairbanks told me," Sherri answered. "He told me about your contacting him."

Josh smiled, obviously pleased that his grandfather had acknowledged his presence to someone. "You're right about the arrival date," he admitted. "But the job I was working on finished early, so I decided not to wait any longer. When I got to town, my grandfather was gone, and since I needed money to finance a place to stay while I waited for him, I took the job. You see, Mrs. Kirk, my landlady, owns the station, and needed some help, so it was a natural fit."

Josh reached for his wallet, and drew from it a worn

snapshot which he pushed across the table to Sherri. "It's my grandfather with my dad. Dad died when I was just a month old, so until now, that snapshot has been the only tangible tie to either of these men I was named for."

Sherri studied the picture closely. Although it was a man in his mid-fifties standing beside a teenage boy, there was no mistaking the firm chin, and the wide, heavy brows over deep-set eyes that characterized the elderly Joshua Fairbanks she had known.

She smiled as she handed the photo back to Josh. "Now I know why you seemed familiar to me when I first saw you at the gas pump. You have the same chin, the same eyes and brows as your grandfather. His were nice eyes, kind and thoughtful. You can be glad you resemble him in that way." Josh grinned his appreciation.

"Wait a minute, Sherri," Josh brightened as the realization hit him. "If you've just been with my grandfather, then you know when he's coming. I can't believe the meeting I've waited for is almost here."

"Oh, Josh!" Sherri's shoulders sagged as the weight of the news she was going to have to share pressed on her. Josh would have to know Mr. Fairbanks had died. And there was no one to tell him but her.

"Josh, I don't know how to tell you," she began softly. "I didn't say anything before because I didn't know you were his grandson."

Josh looked at her and waited. "What is it? What's wrong?"

Sherri slipped her hand over Josh's in an attempt to soften the blow. "Your grandfather . . . he's dead. I'm so sorry."

Josh looked at her in disbelief, then the realization of what she had just said sank in. "He's dead? How did it happen?"

"What I told you about his being bedfast was true.

That's how we met. I cared for him in his apartment. He seemed to be doing so well, but the night after I left for vacation, he suffered a massive heart attack and died."

Josh walked to the kitchen window and peered out into the darkness. "I was so close to meeting him. I was so excited when I found his name among Dad's papers. I thought knowing him would help me put together the pieces of my dad's life. My mother had promised my dad before he died that she'd get me here for a visit. Now I can't keep her promise, either."

Josh shook his head and leaned against the sink. "Now he'll never know what it meant to me to meet him, even if he wasn't interested in a relationship with me."

Sherri got up from the table and moved to stand beside him at the window. When she laid her hand lightly on his arm, he turned toward her. "He did care about you, Josh. I know he did. Even if he'd never seen you, he loved you. That's why he asked me to stop here. He wanted you to know from the moment you arrived how much you mattered to him."

Josh absorbed her words. "Is what you're saying true? If it is, you've just given me the nicest gift I've ever received. It means there was a bond of caring between my grandfather and me, even though we were both unaware of how the other felt. Knowing that makes the disappointment of his death easier to bear. Thank you, Sherri." And he hugged her for a moment.

"Now. Sit down," he told her. "Tell me about him."

As they sat together at the kitchen table, Sherri went back over the last weeks with Mr. Fairbanks. As she described him to Josh, she warmed again at the memory of his humor and his gentle concern for her. She recounted for Josh the peace that would come into his eyes as she responded to his request to read from the Bible.

"It wasn't just religious rules, or beautiful words to

him," she told Josh. "It was as though he was hearing a letter from his best friend."

"It means so much to hear that," Josh told her, "because my relationship with Jesus Christ is very important to me, too. I had hoped my grandfather would be a Christian, and now it sounds as if he was."

"Oh, he was," Sherri affirmed. "And he was quick to ask about my relationship with God, too. He seemed so glad when I told him that I'd asked Jesus to forgive my sins and be my Savior back when I was in junior high."

Josh's eyes brightened. "You're a Christian, too?"

"I am," she said slowly, "but not the way your grandfather was. Jesus was such a vital part of his daily life. It was like that for me at first, I guess, but my parents were killed in a car accident. I couldn't understand why. If God is so powerful and loving, why did they have to die? Why did He let it happen? I decided anyone who would treat good people like that wasn't worthy of my trust."

Was it disappointment she read in Josh's expression, or sympathy? She wasn't sure.

"Oh, Sherri, I know how you feel. I struggled with those same doubts, especially about having to grow up without a dad. But God doesn't bring hurt to us."

Sherri went on as if she hadn't heard him. "What's happened to your grandfather just proves it. He loved Jesus, yet he dies within a few days of fulfilling a life dream." The anger in her voice was evident.

"Trusting Jesus won't always take away the pain in life, but it sure does make the pain easier to bear," Josh returned gently.

Sherri looked at him for a long moment, and the anger she felt dissipated as she saw the compassion in his eyes. "Forgive me. I'm glad for the peace you've found in trusting Jesus. I envy you for being able to believe Him. I'm sorry for pushing my frustration on you, especially with the disappointment you must be feeling now. I should be trying to comfort you, instead of the other way around."

"We don't have to solve everything tonight, do we?" he smiled at her, and stood to stretch. The rain had quieted to a gentle steady rhythm, and the house seemed to have lost much of its foreboding for Sherri. Suddenly she felt very tired, and a long yawn escaped her lips.

"Looks like you are ready for bed," Josh observed. "Would you like me to spend the night?"

Sherri sat up, erect. "What?"

Josh laughed. "No, I didn't mean that like it sounded. I just wondered if you'd feel safer if you weren't here alone. A house this size must have plenty of guest rooms, so I'm sure I could find a place to bunk. You wouldn't even know I was here."

She shook her head. "I'll be fine. Really. I'm sure your landlady would worry if you didn't come back tonight, and with the phones out, we have no way of letting her know where you are. Besides, even though I trust you, I'm not sure I'm comfortable with how it would look to have you here."

"All right," he relented and they started for the front door together. "But you will let me take you to breakfast tomorrow, won't you?"

"I'd like that," she responded warmly. "I'll meet you at the station in the morning."

"There is just one more problem, then. I don't have transportation back to town, at least not yet. I hitched a ride out here with a neighbor who let me off down at the foot of the drive. That's why I was so wet when I arrived. But I know Mr. Morrow lives just over the hill. I can ask him for a lift back into town. We haven't met, but people around here seem willing to lend a hand when you need it."

"All right, then. Good-night," Sherri said as she opened the front door.

Josh flashed a grin, then waved as he stepped off the veranda into the night.

Sherri leaned against the closed door a moment. She'd known this man only a few hours, yet she felt safe with him. And maybe what he had to say about God's comfort in our suffering was right. At least it would be worth thinking more about. She reached for the light switch in the hall, then hurried up the dark stairs toward the lamp's glow that beckoned her from her opened bedroom door.

As she turned down the bedcovers, a rumble of thunder caught her attention. The storm sounded like it was picking up again. She parted the draperies to look out the window, and as she did, she remembered the curtain she had noticed blowing out the open window when she first drove up.

Oh, dear, she thought, *it was raining so hard, something in the room may have gotten wet. And it's still raining fairly steady. I suppose I should close that window.*

Sherri slipped into her robe and slippers again, and lamp in hand, stepped into the hallway. "Let's see," she said half-aloud. "The room was near the center of the house, so it shouldn't be far from here. My room faces away from the drive, so it would have to be on the opposite side of the hall."

She had guessed correctly. As she stood before the heavy door just down the hall opposite hers, she could feel cold air against her ankles. A window was open inside. She turned the knob, but the door was locked.

Then she remembered the extra key on the house-key ring Mr. Fairbanks had given her. She retrieved it from her room, and inserted it in the door. The key fit perfectly. Then turning the knob, she gave the heavy door a push.

As she stepped through the partially open door, a flash of lightning cut the darkness and lighted her way for an instant toward the open window. Rain was blowing into some old books piled on a chaise near the window. "Not the books," Sherri groaned. "Knowing this house, they're probably collectors' items." But as she hurried across the room toward them, she stumbled over something, and fell headlong. Starting to rise, she half turned to see what had caused her to trip.

Her breath caught in a sudden gasp of horror. She heard someone begin to scream, over and over, and the sound filled her ears, pulsating within her head.

Unable to move, paralyzed with fear, her terror-filled eyes stared at the crumpled form of a gray-haired woman.

After what seemed endless time, she wrenched her gaze from the staring eyes, the drying blood that half covered the inert face.

Stumbling frantically to her feet, forgetting the beating rain, the open window, she picked her way back around the lifeless form, knowing that the screams she'd heard had been her own.

Grabbing the door, she slammed it quickly behind her. Her breath seemed to tear at her throat. She felt her legs and feet moving as though in slow motion over the hall carpet toward the door of her room.

Back inside her room, panic hit full force. There was a murderer in the house, and she was alone! She grabbed her purse and overnight case and ran for the stairs. Halfway down, she tripped on the hem of her robe, and half slid, half ran the rest of the way down. As she reached the door, her overnight case slipped from her grasp, and she lunged forward to push it aside so she could pull open the door. As she bent over, the door burst open from the outside, knocking her down.

With chilling fear her gaze fell on a man's shoes, his pantlegs. Then she was grabbed by two strong hands. Her terrified consciousness could bear no more and she slid into blackness.

5

From somewhere far away, Sherri heard her name being called, but she didn't want to open her eyes. She wanted to sleep, to keep a horrible, nameless something away.

But the voice was insistent, "Sherri, Sherri; it's all right. Don't be frightened."

The voice was familiar. Then she felt herself held firmly, gently.

"Sherri, please. Open your eyes."

She forced her lids open and found the deep, gray eyes of Josh Stevens just a foot from her own.

His arm was holding her, his wet clothing soaking through her robe. She realized she was on the foyer floor with her overnight case under one hip and Josh was on one knee, supporting her with an arm under her shoulders.

She shook her head to clear away the fog, then allowed him to pull her to her feet.

"Sherri, what happened? What's wrong?"

She reached out both hands, her face twisting like a little girl's in fear and near tears. Then she felt his arms firm about her and she sobbed against his chest.

He held her close as she clung to him. "It'll be all right, Sherri," he murmured softly. "Whatever it is, it'll be all right."

"Oh, Josh," she choked out between sobs, "I was so frightened. I didn't know what to do."

"What were you frightened about?"

"I saw . . . upstairs. Oh, it was horrible!"

"What was?"

"I saw someone lying on the floor, maybe the housekeeper. She looked like she was dead. She's been murdered."

"What!"

"When I went upstairs after you left, I remembered noticing a window open when I arrived, so I went to close it. I thought the rain would be blowing in." Her voice started to falter and she began to tremble.

"And I fell over her." Sherri's voice choked with the memory. "Josh, we have to call the police." Then Sherri groaned and pulled away from him as she remembered that the phones were dead because of the storm.

"We've got to keep our heads," Josh said firmly, looking behind Sherri and up the dark staircase. "First, that woman . . . Sherri, are you sure she was dead?"

Sherri pushed her hair back from her face. "I think so. She didn't move or make a sound. But I was with her only a moment."

"I need to be sure," Josh said. "We can't call for help, and if she's badly injured and unconscious, she may die before we get back here with a doctor. I'll have a look and you stay here."

Sherri's voice took on a new resolution. "I'm going with you, Josh. I'm a nurse. If she needs attention, I'll know what to do."

"But this could be very dangerous," Josh protested. "If someone killed her, he may still be up there."

"Not much more dangerous than staying here alone," Sherri argued. "No, I'm going with you."

"All right," Josh relented, "but we're not attempting this without weapons. This is the time that knife from the kitchen might come in handy. We'll go there first."

Taking Sherri firmly by the hand, and reaching for his

pocket flashlight with the other, Josh led the way back to the darkened kitchen and found the knife. Then the two crept up the long staircase toward the glow of the lamp Sherri had left on the table in the hall.

As they approached the darkened doorway, Josh motioned Sherri back against the wall as he inched up and cautiously peered into the room. Nothing stirred, so tightening his grip on the knife handle, Josh moved into the doorway and shined his flashlight across the floor.

"Sherri," he called softly. "Sherri, there's no one here."

"What?" Sherri joined him, and watched as he moved the flashlight back and forth across the floor. She realized in horror that the body was gone!

She gripped Josh's arm. "She was right over there, right at the foot of the chaise. I *know* she was." Terror and confusion rose in Sherri's voice. "What could have happened?"

"Are you sure this is the same room?" Josh asked.

"This is the room," Sherri insisted. "The room where I'm staying is on the opposite side and just down the hall."

Josh turned to look her in the eyes. "Then, are you sure about the body? I mean, are you really sure you saw a dead woman? There's no chance, is there, that you could have fallen asleep and had a very vivid dream?"

"I *know* it wasn't a dream," she pleaded. "Please believe me."

Josh looked down at her for a moment, then took her arm and guided her toward the door. "Why don't I take a look around the place? You get dressed, meet me in the kitchen, and we'll decide what to do after that."

Sherri went with him to collect her belongings at the bottom of the stairs, then he left her in her room while he checked the mansion for signs of forced entry.

Sherri dressed slowly, breathing deeply and trying to relax. She made her way to the kitchen and waited quietly for Josh, her muscles still tense. Finally, Josh came in through the back door, startling her a little. He laid the knife back in its place on the bread tray and slipped his flashlight back into his pocket. Sherri waited wordlessly for his report, but he just shook his head. "I couldn't find a thing amiss," he told her. "Nothing unusual in any room I checked, and no sign outside of anything being wrong."

Sherri sank down into the chair by the kitchen table. She was sure she had seen the dead woman. *But could I have become so unnerved by this solitary, stormy night that I did imagine a horrible phantom?* she wondered.

Josh moved to her side and gently patted her shoulder. "Let's heat up that coffee and try to think clearly about this. Maybe there's some logical explanation for what you think you saw."

Then seeing her irritated look, he said, "Sorry, I mean, for what you saw. We found no woman, though, Sherri."

"But she was there, Josh," Sherri insisted again, as she rose to start a fresh pot of coffee.

Measuring the grounds into the percolator top, she said, "I don't understand it. I just can't understand what's happened."

Neither spoke for a moment as Josh got cups and saucers and Sherri brought the cream and sugar. He held out a chair for her. "Let's try to figure this out, Sherri. I honestly don't feel you're the type of person who is prone to wild imaginings. But sometimes, under circumstances that are already unsettling, items in an unfamiliar room can seem to take on other characteristics. Could that have happened, do you think? Is there any possibility in your mind that you didn't see what you thought you did?"

Sherri stood and went to the stove where the coffee was already sending out steam with its aroma. She extinguished the flame and carried the pot to the table. Deliberately, slowly, she poured the coffee, then sat down.

Looking directly into his eyes, hers flashing with suppressed irritation and fear, Sherri said, "I stumbled and fell over something. When I started to get up, an especially bright streak of lightning illuminated the entire room."

Sherri paused, taking a quick sip of the hot coffee. "I saw a middle-aged, almost elderly woman on the floor. I'm sure she was dead." Sherri shivered with the memory. "Her eyes were staring blankly, and there was blood on her face. She was wearing a blue dress. I could see the definite blue even in that short moment. She was there. And I'm sure she was dead. I did *not* imagine it!"

She looked down at her cup and curled both hands around it. Her fingers felt very cold.

"I believe you, Sherri. She wasn't there when I searched, but I believe you."

"I believe you because there are pieces to this puzzle that haven't all fit into place."

Sherri took a swallow of her coffee, then looked at him, confused. "What are you talking about, Josh?"

"I'm talking about your car," he answered. "Sherri, did you have car trouble after you left the service station this afternoon?"

"No, why?"

Josh raised his eyebrows. "Because when I left here to-night, I noticed that the hood was slightly up on your car. I was surprised anything might be wrong, because when I checked it at the station this afternoon, everything was fine. So I went over to take a look. Sherri, the spark plug wires had been disconnected. It was hard to see with just the flash-light, but I'm sure they had been yanked loose. I was trying to make sense out of what had happened to your car when I heard you screaming, and came inside. I believe you are right about strange goings-on here, but I can't make sense out of who or when."

Sherri caught her breath sharply, and stared at him wide-eyed.

"I think I know," she told him. "Earlier this evening, before you came, I heard a car and went to the door. I assumed it was the housekeeper returning. But a car with its lights off was driving away in the dark. I think I must have been noticed in the doorway, because suddenly it picked up speed and disappeared."

"Why didn't you tell me this before?" Josh asked sharply.

"I wasn't really sure at first if it was important," Sherri said. She hesitated, then went on quietly, "And I had no way of knowing whether or not it might have been you in the car."

"No wonder you were suspicious of me earlier," he said, leaning back in his chair. "And I can't blame you. You had no reason to trust me." Then he paused, and got up to refill his coffee cup. "But why would someone be prowling around here? No one knows you are here, and no one in this town would have a reason to hurt me." Josh added with a laugh, "I certainly don't own any valuables anyone would want!"

Valuables. In the excitement of the evening, Sherri had forgotten to tell him about the things his grandfather had sent him. "Oh, Josh, you do own valuables, at least they were valuables to your grandfather. He gave them to me to give to you. There's a watch, Josh, and a key. There's a letter for you, too. Though it's here in the house, I haven't located it yet."

The events of the night had taken their toll on Sherri, and now that the immediate danger seemed to have passed, she suddenly felt very tired.

"You've had about enough for one night," he smiled at her. "There'll be time tomorrow to find the letter. As soon as it's light, I'll see what else someone might have done to your car, but until then, there's not much we can do, and I think we're safe here for now. You must have forgotten to lock the doors before, so I'll check them now to make sure they're secure. Why don't you try to get some rest?"

Sherri was too tired to protest, so she followed meekly as he walked her to her room. "If it makes you rest easier, lock your door," he instructed Sherri. "But don't worry. I'll be nearby, and nothing's going to happen to you."

———

The sun was filtering through the filmy lace curtains and her watch showed it was almost nine when Sherri awoke. She'd slept soundly, although she hadn't expected to even fall asleep.

Quickly washing her face and brushing her hair, she dressed and went to look for Josh.

Somehow the fear she had experienced in this house seemed unreal, far away, and she felt a sense of elation as she stepped lightly down the staircase.

A shaft of sunlight shone through the front entrance fanlight, washing the marble floor below in warmth. Reaching the foyer, she called Josh's name; then deciding he must be upstairs, she started back up.

"Are you looking for someone?" Sherri froze. It was a man's voice coming from the foyer, but it was definitely not Josh's.

Sherri turned slowly, gripping the railing.

A red-haired young man with an armload of logs had entered from the dining room area and stood looking up at her.

"Who are you?" she asked waveringly.

"Arnie Morrow. Who are you?"

The housekeeper's son? The terror of the night before momentarily gripped her again, and she answered hesitatingly, "I'm Sherri McElroy, a friend of Mr. Fairbanks."

"Well, Fairbanks is out of town for a while. I'm not sure when he'll be back. Give me a minute to get rid of these logs." Arnie went into the library off the foyer and Sherri came back down the stairs. She followed him partway into the room. As he arranged the firewood on the hearth, she asked haltingly, "Your mother, where is she?"

"Over at our house, I suppose. She generally comes later in the day when Fairbanks isn't home. I'm just getting in myself, but I remembered Mom wanted this ready today in case the old man arrives. Gets a bit cool here some spring evenings. I'm not sure when she expects him."

Sherri began to feel uneasy, "You said you were just getting in. When did you talk with your mother?"

"Yesterday morning before I left for Pikestown. A friend of ours needed help. We worked so late, I just stayed all night." He stood, and turning, smiled at her. "Since Mr. Fairbanks isn't here, as far as I know, can I do anything for you?"

"No, thank you," Sherri answered carefully. "I'm just here to pick up something for him. I can take care of it."

"Okay," Arnie said, dusting his hands together, "then I'll just get on home and see what work is lined up for today.

"I'm on vacation from my college classes this week," he added as he crossed the foyer, "so I'm helping Dad with some work around the grounds."

"Is he Mr. Fairbanks' caretaker?" Sherri asked.

"Right," Arnie said as he started out the door. "See you later, maybe. Sherri McElroy, was it?"

Sherri nodded, and as the door shut behind him, she wished Josh were with her. "Where is he anyway?" she muttered with a tinge of exasperation. "I want to get finished and away from here—whether there's a body around here or not."

She decided to find Mr. Fairbanks' desk and have the letter ready for Josh, unless he was at her room already looking for her.

She went back upstairs again and called lightly, "Josh?"

Receiving no answer, she looked into the two rooms next to hers on the left.

Glancing in, she discovered a nursery and adjacent to it, a large playroom.

"Most of the things in here must be well over a hundred years old," she mused. "I wish I had time to browse a while; it looks like it would be fun."

The room that had so terrified her last night was directly across from the playroom, and Sherri considered bypassing it and continuing her search elsewhere. But then she stopped. Josh had said there was nothing to fear there, and besides, confronting the scene of her terror might wash away the uneasiness that clung to her.

Though the door was closed, the key was still where she'd left it in the lock. It turned easily and she entered a room bathed in sunshine, this time placing the key in her pocket. Josh had been right. There were no signs of anything foreboding here, only an inviting, pleasant study. The room was paneled in warm, dark wood, with deep shelves lining two walls. The shelves held rows of thick, leather-bound volumes interspersed with pieces of sculpture and family photos.

Then she spied the desk. It dominated the end of the room, imposing beneath a magnificent leaded-glass window. Could this have been the desk Mr. Fairbanks had meant?

Sherri crossed the room to it, her steps cushioned in the thick Persian rug. But before she could reach out to open the drawers, a harsh, unfamiliar male voice shattered the silence. "What are you doing in there?"

Sherri whirled, her heart pounding.

6

"I said, what are you doing!" The rasping voice belonged to a powerfully built middle-aged man. From across the room, the non-color of his hair made him seem to be without eyebrows, and its wispiness raised his high, thin forehead even higher. As he came toward her with a slow, menacing gait, she saw his eyes, a strange red-brown. She recognized him from her gas-station stop the day before as the angry man who had pulled up just as she was leaving.

Sherri was frightened. A vivid picture of the body of the night before flashed across her mind, but she knew she must appear calm.

"I might ask the same of you. Who are you?"

"Frank Dodson, Fairbanks' attorney, if that's any of your business, young lady."

Sherri felt relieved at his identification, though a bit irritated at his arrogance. "Oh, I'm sorry, Mr. Dodson. I'm Sherri McElroy from New York. I've been Mr. Fairbanks' private nurse the last few weeks. He asked me to stop and get something for him, since I was coming this way."

A sudden glint appeared in Dodson's eyes and she saw a quick flash of interest which was quickly concealed behind an effusive joviality. "Oh, Miss McElroy. You say he's been ill? I hadn't been notified. And he's getting along well, I suppose? Good of you to feel friendly toward him. And what did you say he sent you for?"

Dodson had advanced toward her and now had a seemingly casual but firm grip on her arm. She could feel the blunt fingertips pressing into her flesh.

"Come with me. This is such a depressing room, don't you agree?" he said, the pressure he exerted on her arm forcing her to turn toward the door.

His voice and his manner repelled her, but she smiled politely, unobtrusively trying to slip from his grasp as she was propelled along beside him.

Once in the hall, after closing the door behind them, he asked piercingly, "And how did you get in there? I thought that room was always kept locked." Quickly he pasted on a thin smile above his jowled chin.

"Oh, really?" Sherri said innocently. "The door opened easily for me. When I saw that lovely desk, I just had to get a closer look. I just love the lines of old furniture, don't you?" She hoped her chatter would quiet any suspicions he might have.

But Frank Dodson was not so easily dissuaded. "And what, may I ask," he questioned, almost too casually, "did you intend to get for Mr. Fairbanks? Perhaps I can help you."

Was she being overcautious because of her dislike for this man? She deliberated swiftly, then responded, "Oh, it's really nothing of consequence, Mr. Dodson," she said sweetly, "but it did seem important to Mr. Fairbanks. And since I was coming this way anyhow, I thought I'd indulge his request."

Sherri kept her voice light as she continued, watching Dodson's reaction carefully. "While he was hospitalized he met this little boy from the pediatrics ward and thought it would be nice to give him one of the antique toys from the old playroom here."

Sherri saw his obvious relief as he loosened his grip on her arm. "It's right across the hall," she added brightly.

Slipping out of his grasp, she went into the playroom

and pretended to browse among the rows of toys on the shelves.

"Which do you think would be best?" she asked, turning. Sherri was uncomfortable lying about her reason for being here, but she felt wary of this man.

"Mr. Dodson, what do you think?" she asked again as he stood in the doorway, seemingly lost in thought.

"Oh, ah, I'm sure whatever you choose will be fine," he said vacantly, "just fine," and turning, he headed down the hall.

Sherri started after him. "What did you come for, Mr. Dodson? Is it anything I can help you with?"

He stopped abruptly and turned, rubbing his hands together slowly, "Er, ah, no . . . I can take care of it later. Do you intend to be here long?"

Still cautious, Sherri answered, "This shouldn't take long at all."

"Well then, good day," Dodson said. "You needn't see me out." And with that, he continued down the hall and disappeared down the stairs. A few moments later she heard his heavy footsteps on the foyer floor, then the soft thud of the front door closing.

Sherri quickly turned back to the study, wondering why Dodson made her so uneasy. Pulling out the large leather chair behind the desk, she sat down.

Sunlight sparkled down over her shoulders onto the desktop from the window behind her.

Like everything else in this fine old house, the desktop held a few well-chosen, quality accessories: A leather-edged blotter, an old-fashioned pen beside a silver inkwell, a heavy silver paperweight resting on a few scribbled notes, and a small oval, silver frame, containing the image of a beautiful young woman in a high-necked blouse, blond hair piled on top of her head.

"I wonder who she was," Sherri murmured, turning it

over to see if there might be a notation as to her identity. Scratched into the back of the frame were a strange combination of letters and a number, DR–R–3.

She placed it back on the desk, her thoughts reverting to the habit of a childhood hide-and-seek word game that her grandfather had played with her many times. "DR . . . R . . . 3 . . . hmm . . ."

Sherri wondered if she should wait for Josh before looking through this desk for the letter his grandfather wanted him to have. *But Mr. Fairbanks did ask me to find it,* she thought, *so I suppose it's okay; and the sooner I find the letter, the sooner I can be on my way.*

The thought of leaving should have pleased her, but at the same time, she disliked leaving Josh. *I've known him only a short time,* she thought, as she began her search through the drawers on the right side of the desk, *but he's certainly won my respect.*

She found nothing but neatly filed statements and other business papers in those drawers.

The wide, shallow center drawer of the desk held plain white stationery, stamps, and an address book, all placed tidily side by side. "He certainly was an orderly man," she murmured to herself. "No wonder he had such a clear mind at the end. At least I hope it was unclouded. I wouldn't want to be hunting for a letter that doesn't exist. But Josh is real. At least that part of Mr. Fairbanks' story is true."

The left bank of drawers seemed to contain only stacks of letters, some bound with navy blue ribbon, some with red, but none addressed to Josh. There were also various-sized boxes, some velvet, some of carved wood, others of ivory. All of the drawers contained what seemed to be personal mementoes—all except the third drawer, which came out only about three-fourths as far as the others, no matter how firmly she pulled. *It's probably stuck from old age,* Sherri thought. It seemed empty anyway except for the thin leather-bound book lying alone in the bottom of the wide drawer.

Taking the little book in her lap and opening it on the desktop, she read aloud what was written there following the date, July 9, 1966. "On this day my son left home; may God go with him."

Sherri quickly turned to the next page. The entry was headed by a date several years later than the first. "This day is a special one—I learned that I am a grandfather," it read. "May God grant that one day that boy, my son's son, will sit behind this desk and know its secrets."

Sherri flipped the pages carefully to where a ribbon marked a page near the back of the book. It was headed by a fairly recent date. She read, "My grandson has contacted me! Today I leave for New York to retrieve the portion of his legacy I have kept there. Many years of prayers are soon to be answered."

She slipped the little book back into the drawer, thinking, *Josh will undoubtedly be delighted to see this.*

As she started to shut the drawer, something nagged at her mind. *Why should the notation on that picture frame remind me of something?*

Sherri stood up, and reaching across the wide desk, she picked up the picture again and turned it over in her hands. The brightness of the sunlight through the bevels of the window behind her cast a soft glow over the burnished frame. The carefully scratched inscription was clearly visible now, and she stared intently at it, searching her memory. "What is there about it?" she wondered half-aloud. "Why do I feel I've seen it, or part of it, before?" But whatever was familiar about it eluded her.

As she was replacing the frame on the desk, she suddenly gasped, "Of course, that's it! The watch!" She scrutinized the inscription again, then ran quickly to her room for her purse and small leather bag Mr. Fairbanks had given her.

Back in the study, she pulled out the heavy gold watch and carefully pushed the tiny catch that flipped the cover open, revealing the watch's face and the inside of its cover.

Holding it beside the frame, she compared the notations scratched on each, "DR–R–3." She made out an additional inscription in the watch, "Job 38:22."

"They *are* the same!" she exclaimed. "But what's the connection between the watch and this photo?"

She sat down, holding the frame and the watch in her lap. "The watch inscription is a reference to something in the Bible," she murmured to herself, "but what does DR–R–3 represent?"

She turned possibilities over in her mind. "It could be a serial number of something, or perhaps a filing symbol."

Opening the right-hand desk drawers, she specifically noted the types of papers stored there. They all seemed to be general business transactions, with no filing tabs or codes similar to the DR-R-3. Perhaps the odd alphabet and digit sequence could pertain to something in the ribbon-bound letters or the accumulation of boxes. But if so, what?

"Let's see, now, a dash represents something connecting or missing." Sherri's mind followed avenues of speculation for some moments as she sounded aloud the phonics of the engraved consonants, "Dr'r, Drr," then added vowels, "Drar, Dreer, Drir, Dror."

Sherri jumped up. "Dror! Drawer, drawer three. Hm, drawer-R-three—drawer right three. That's it, the third drawer on the right. That could be it!"

Trying to be calm, she sat down again and reopened the third drawer on the right side. She checked through the ledgers and file cards again, more carefully now, looking for some clue. She realized that in her excitement, she might be overlooking the very thing she was hunting. But there was nothing obvious to her that would have any special significance.

She sat back dejectedly. "Oh, well, it probably hasn't anything to do with Josh anyway," she mused. "But I still haven't found the letter I'm to give to him. Mr. Fairbanks did say the desk in his study, and the extra key did fit the door to this room."

Sherri pivoted suddenly, reaching for the bottom drawer on the left. "Good grief, I haven't checked this one at all!" she exclaimed to herself. "I got sidetracked with that diary and forgot I hadn't opened this last drawer." She shut it again after finding only some very old photograph albums.

She decided to see if she could locate Josh. Remembering that she had noticed a third floor to the huge residence when she arrived, she thought that perhaps he had gone there.

Sherri started to rise, then sat down very suddenly as the phrase "third floor" made her think *third drawer.*

"How stupid of me. What about the left drawers?" she said aloud as she grasped the heavily carved pull of the third drawer on the left. As before, it opened only partway, but far enough to expose the expanse of emptiness where the leather-covered diary had been kept.

Quickly she reached back into the empty drawer, searching for some sort of catch or mechanism that would release it farther.

"Nothing," she said to herself, slumping into the chair in discouragement.

Then bending forward, she probed carefully on the drawer's underside. Her fingers passed over, then returned to, an unobtrusive metal protrusion. It was very smooth, almost indiscernible. Sherri pushed it firmly as she pulled on the drawer.

It slid effortlessly and she looked down into it with elation. There was the letter!

The angular script she had seen in the diary stated, "For *my* grandson, Joshua." Beneath it the same statement, "For my grandson, Joshua," appeared in a different handwriting.

Sherri pulled the drawer out farther and reached forward to take the letter. As she did, the watch slipped from her lap to the floor and slid under the open drawer. She got down on her knees to retrieve it and then slipped it back into the leather case.

Still on her knees, she reached into the drawer for the letter.

As she pulled it out, a glint in the far corner of the compartment caught her eye. She tucked the letter into the pouch with the gold watch, and began to inspect the open drawer's housing.

The glint she had seen in the back corner appeared to be a large keyhole, revealed through a hole cut out of the top edge of the drawer when it was pulled out to its full extension.

Sherri's breath caught with excitement. Her mind darted to the key that Mr. Fairbanks had given to her, the large watch fob key that was now on a fine chain around her neck.

Reaching into the neckline of her sweater, she pulled out the chain. In her hurry to slip it over her head, it tangled in her hair, but she loosened it carefully, impatient with herself, then tried the key in the obscure keyhole.

After a great deal of difficulty, she felt it turn very slowly. It probably allows this drawer to come out, she decided, giving the drawer a firm tug.

Nothing happened. *That's strange,* Sherri thought, perplexed.

Then, hearing a sound as though someone were opening a stubborn door, she quickly slipped the chain and key into the leather pouch. Remembering her distrust of Frank Dodson, she scrambled to her feet and concealed the pouch behind her. She was surprised to see that no one was there, and a slight prickle moved up and down her spine.

Telling herself to be sensible and not afraid of every sound, she turned back to be sure the desk had been left as she found it. As she did so, she noticed that a nearby section of bookshelves seemed to be awry, angled out from the wall about a foot. *Strange I didn't notice that before,* she thought as she stepped toward them. Why had this section of shelves been moved out of line with the others?

She grasped the edge of the unit, and feeling it budge a little, she tugged harder.

To her surprise it swung open like a door, and she stared into a narrow six-foot-high passageway within the wall. She stepped aside to let the light from the window illuminate the interior. This house was certainly full of surprises!

Sherri saw the smooth, but unpolished, wood floor and a portion of the plain walls which smelled of cedar. Several wooden pegs protruded from the wall beneath a narrow shelf on which lay an oblong metal box. Her curiosity aroused further, she stepped through the opening and lifted the box's lid. Inside were a number of long, thick candles and a slim glass container of matches.

Eager for a better look, she picked up a candle and struck one of the matches. The flame flared readily from the candle, so she blew out the match's flame and put the blackened stub into a metal saucer on the shelf. Her excitement mounted as she looked around.

The light revealed an empty passageway about ten feet long. At the other end, an enclosed stone stairway led downward.

A secret tunnel! It was like a detail from one of her favorite childhood stories, and certainly too exciting not to explore! The flickering light of the candle lighting her way, she started carefully down.

Instead of reaching a basement as she had expected at the bottom of the steps, she found herself in a narrow, damp rock passageway, an extension of the stairway-tunnel.

She hesitated, vascillating between going back for Josh or venturing farther. She'd look just a little farther, she decided, then go tell Josh what she'd found.

The atmosphere began to seem more humid as the floor sloped continually downward with an occasional rough step carved out to lessen the sharp descent. The passage appeared to have been cut from the rock surrounding it.

Then suddenly, the passageway leveled out and she was able to glance around without fearing for her footing. The area had widened considerably and she saw several formations of some sort of rock along the floor. *This looks almost like a cave of some sort*, Sherri thought.

But as she reached the far end of the large oval room, she discovered that it wasn't just an isolated cave. At one end two corridors angled off in roughly opposite directions. Since her candle was giving a nice little circle of light, she decided to walk a short way down one of the passages.

The floor of this section was strewn with rocks of various sizes and she felt a cooling of the air. Then the candle-flame began flickering, and suddenly Sherri remembered how last night she'd stood holding a flickering lamp outside the door of the room—*that* room.

Sherri turned quickly to go back, terror beginning to mount as the vivid memory of the dead woman flashed across her mind.

At that moment, she felt a sharp draft and the flame went out. She was engulfed in intense blackness such as she had never before experienced.

Stifling a cry, Sherri hesitated, fighting an overwhelming fear.

"It's your own fault that you're in this position," she scolded herself. "You should have waited for Josh. Now just be sensible and think."

Sherri stood motionless, trying to get her bearings, feeling that surely there must be unseen eyes watching her, unseen hands reaching out for her. Her skin crawled.

With all her mental strength she pushed the imaginings away, choking down a cry of panic.

She concentrated, trying to remember exactly where she was standing. She knew the passage had been about eight feet wide. "If I turn around about another quarter turn, then go forward approximately four or five steps, I should find the wall and can follow it back."

Sherri was shivering now, but she tried to forget her fear and turned a bit, very slowly, and stepped forward, then took a small, cautious step. As she stepped out again, her toe caught on a rock and she fell forward, scraping her hands and knees.

Her cry of fear and exasperation changed to one of relief as her groping hands touched the rock wall.

Scrambling to her feet and keeping close to the wall, she inched along over the scattered stones.

After a short interval, the floor seemed to be without any obstacles and she moved more quickly, her breath coming in short sobs of relief. Surely she must be approaching the passage that led to the stairs.

The wall felt increasingly damp and she started when something quick and light ran across her hand. But she was afraid to move away, fearful of losing her bearings again.

She hurried as fast as she could in the total blackness, arms outstretched, one hand moving along the wall, the other stretched out in front of her to protect against running into anything.

There was a definite draft against her legs now. Sure it was from the open entry into the house above, she stepped forward in haste, breathing a sigh of thanksgiving.

Then, suddenly she was slipping, sliding, falling downward through space.

7

*S*herri's head banged against something as she crashed to a sudden, awkward, skidding halt, and she sank into a blackness deeper than the tangible one which surrounded her.

She regained consciousness with the sense of being engulfed in pain and darkness, and with the faint sound of softly moving water.

Sherri lay quietly, trying to remember where she was, wondering why she had such a severe headache.

She stretched her eyes open wide, but was unable to see. Then trying to get up, she felt the clammy rock floor beneath her. *Oh, no!* she thought, memory rushing back, *I must have fallen into some sort of pit.*

The reality of the danger she faced flooded over her. She felt a new fear mounting deep within, worse than the fear she'd experienced earlier. *What if I can't find a way out? What if no one finds me! No one but Josh is in the house, and I haven't seen him all morning. What if he left? What if . . .*

Sherri hugged her knees to her chest to protect herself from the darkness and began to sob. "Jesus! God! Are you listening? Please help me . . . please . . ."

As she pleaded, it was as if strong, quieting arms had gathered her close; and in the darkness, she felt as though she was not alone.

Her breathing was steadier now, and she sat quietly for a few moments, wondering what to do. She could try to find a wall, as she had before, and follow it. Of course she'd just tried that, and it landed her here instead of close to safety.

Maybe the water she heard running could offer a way out. An underground stream had to start somewhere. If she could find it and follow it, maybe it would lead her out of here.

Leaning back on her heels, she tried to distinguish the water sound.

Too shaky to stand, she raised herself to her hands and knees and crawled in what she thought was the direction of the stream. However, she found nothing but more rocky floor.

The pain in her head was starting to befuddle her thinking, and she felt drowsy, her whole body aching, as the darkness began to close in again.

Then she heard it, faintly at first and so indistinct she was sure it must be her imagination.

Sherri strained to listen through the throbbing in her head. A few moments later she heard it again, faint and far away. It sounded like someone calling.

She tensed, listening with every nerve alert. There it was again. She bent her head back and looked up.

Nothing but blackness.

Had the sound been real? Sherri became frightened, realizing she might be having hallucinations from the injury to her head.

But then she saw it, a small blur of faint light far above her. And this time she was sure someone was calling.

"Hello!" she shouted. "Hello! Here! I'm here!"

"Sherri?"

"Yes, yes, it's me. I'm down here!" She scrambled to her feet too quickly and she felt herself swaying as dizziness began to overcome her. She sank to the cold rock floor, straining to keep her sight on the light high above her.

"Be careful!" she cried, gaining new strength. "Stay back!"

"What?"

"Be careful! There's some sort of dropoff, a pit of some kind. I can't tell what it is!"

"I see it!"

Then suddenly the light grew and filled a large round area above her. At its edge she saw a distorted face peering down at her.

Shocked, she wondered if her vision was playing tricks on her.

"Sherri! Sherri?" The voice was Josh's, his face distorted by the shadows cast by the light he held.

"Yes. Do you think you can help me out of here?" Their voices echoed hollowly, thrown back and forth against the rock walls.

"How did you get down there? What happened?"

"I fell. I was exploring, and my candle went out. I lost my way back. How did you ever find me?"

"First let me get you out of there. Are you okay? Were you injured?"

"I seem to be all right, except that my head's pounding and I'm very sore."

"I'll have to leave you alone for a little while while I go for a better light and some rope. I'll be back as quickly as I can."

"All right," she replied tremulously, "but please hurry."

"I will, Sherri. Hang on." Josh and the light vanished, leaving Sherri alone again in the pressing darkness.

As she huddled there, she noticed a bit of light near her hand, then realized it was her luminous watch dial, which up until now had been hidden under her sleeve. She noted with surprise that it was only eleven o'clock.

The waiting seemed long and the darkness even more intense than before. It was only by glancing at her watch occasionally that she had any sense of the passing of time, or any awareness of her location.

But in about half an hour, she again saw above her the glow of light. It became brighter and larger, and then Josh's welcome voice called, "Sherri?"

"Yes, Josh, I'm okay."

Suddenly bright light penetrated almost to where she sat and she heard Josh's long whistle.

"When you pick a place to fall, you go at it in a big way."

From where she sat, up to where Josh peered down at her, sloped a long chute-like tunnel about twenty feet across.

"It must be forty or fifty feet down to where you are, Sherri," he called. "I couldn't find rope or anything else around that will work. Do you see any kind of steps or hand-holds anywhere?"

Sherri turned her gaze and inspected the rock wall of the tunnel above her. It was difficult to discern anything in the mixture of blinding light and wavering shadow, and she was about to tell him she saw no way out. Then he stepped back from the rim, relocating the beam of light, and she saw it.

"Josh, to your right," she called, "about five feet or so. There's a protrusion of some sort. Maybe it's just a rock, but it's just below that spot where the edge bulges out."

The light moved again, Josh appeared above the place she'd pointed out. "Over to your right a bit farther, and below you. You've almost reached whatever it is."

In a few seconds, he gave a shout of accomplishment. "We're in luck! It seems to be a rolled up rope-ladder. Let me make sure it's well secured and in good enough condition to use. If all's well on that score, we'll see how far it reaches."

Shortly, he yelled, "Okay, I'm going to start lowering

it. Stand back in case it falls. It seems all right, but I don't want to chance your getting hurt."

Sherri watched as the ladder descended over the edge, slowly swaying out away from the face of the sloping rock wall. Closer, slowly closer it came, until it was just above her.

"How's it doing?" Josh hollered.

"It's only about two feet above the floor now."

"Do you think you can climb it if I explain how?"

"I don't know, Josh. It doesn't look very steady, and I'm so weak, I'm afraid I'd fall again."

"All right, Sherri, no problem. Just stay out of the way now because I'm coming down for you."

Sherri sank back in relief. But as Josh came over the rim and put a foot on the first rung, the ladder began to sway and jerk. Despite his warning, her concern for him caused her to grab on to the ladder end in both hands, then strain to hold it steady.

The fibers of the rope cut into her hands and the oily, yet heavy dusty smell of it nauseated her. But she held on as best she could, watching above her as the light slowly descended, seeming to shorten the shaft's depth as it came.

The glow was accompanied by the giant crab-like shadow that was Josh, moving slowly downward. When she saw his legs just above her, she loosened her grip on the rope and stepped aside.

Josh descended the last few steps, the rope rungs sagging beneath his weight. Then he was beside her, his arms around her, pulling her close.

Sherri rested against the strong hardness of his chest for a few moments. An hour ago she had feared this moment of safety would never come.

Josh patted her shoulder, then let her go. Shining his floodlight slowly around the cavern in which they stood, it illuminated an immense dome-like room with the chute-tunnel opening almost above its center. "Who would have guessed there'd be a place like this under the house?" he exclaimed.

Sherri started to respond, then reached out to steady herself against him as she felt herself begin to sway.

"Are you all right?" Josh asked, putting one arm around her shoulder and shining the light to see her face.

"You look white, Sherri," he said as she began to murmur an answer. "We'd better get you out of here as quickly as possible."

"I feel dizzy, Josh!" she said slowly. "I honestly don't think I can climb that rope ladder."

"I'll check around and see if I can find another way out so you won't have to," he said. "Here," he added, slipping out of his jacket, "You can sit on this so you won't get as cold."

He arranged it for her and held her hand as she sank to the floor, then taking a small flashlight from his pocket, he handed it to her. After walking the circumference of the field-size room, he disappeared through an opening at the far side.

As Sherri sat with her legs curled beneath her, waiting for him to return, she shuddered at what could have happened to her if he hadn't come. Had her prayer made a difference? Had God heard her and sent Josh to help? She wondered.

Sherri shifted on Josh's jacket, trying to pull it over her legs where her slacks had been torn. Her knees showed through the rends, not bleeding but badly scraped. She was feeling more and more chilled as the minutes passed. Even the long sleeves and high neck of her sweater could no longer insulate her from this bone-chilling cold.

She shoved her hands into her pockets and tried to hunch herself together for warmth.

Even though she was shivering, Sherri realized she was

beginning to feel drowsy. Could she be going into shock?

But then she became aware of a circle of light approaching, and the area around her losing its intense blackness. Josh hurried over to where she was huddled, and asked worriedly, "Sherri, are you feeling worse?"

"About the same," she said, giving him a weak smile. "But I'm so cold, Josh."

Kneeling beside her, he said, "I'm sure you are. I came back as quickly as I could; I'm sorry it was so long. We've got to get you out of here before you develop hypothermia. It sometimes comes on rather quickly following an injury. Sherri, I want you to listen closely to what I'm saying. Our safety depends on it. Do you understand?"

She nodded.

"This area leads to a labyrinth of passages and other cave rooms. There might be another way out, but finding it could take hours. That means," he said slowly, "that we have to go up the ladder."

Sherri twisted, trying to look up at him in the uncertain glow of his light which lay on the floor pointing to a far wall.

But before she could say anything, Josh continued, "We have no choice, because I doubt anyone will discover that we're here."

Sherri shivered, partly from chilling, mostly from fear.

"If you concentrate on what you're doing, the climbing isn't unusually difficult," Josh tried to reassure her. "You must think of nothing but the next step, the next handhold. Do not try to look up to the top or down to me."

"I'll try, Josh," she said quietly.

"All right," he continued, "the important thing to remember is that you don't climb this ladder like you would a regular ladder."

"What other way is there?"

"There's a special technique, similar to what firemen use. I'll explain it to you before we start up. It's fairly simple to do, but very important that you use it. Trying to climb up the regular way causes the ladder to bend horizontally where your weight is placed."

Feeling Sherri tense, Josh said, "But don't worry. I told you only so you'll be careful to do as I show you."

Josh smiled at her and pulled her gently back against him.

"Our heavenly Father," he prayed aloud, "we ask you to watch over us as we make this climb together. Guide each step we take; and enable us to safely reach the top. We thank you, Lord, that you are here with us."

Giving Sherri a gentle hug, Josh got up and helped her to her feet. Picking up his jacket, he slipped it around her. "I want you to put this on and zip it up," he said, helping her. Putting the little flashlight in the jacket pocket and zipping it closed, he picked up the flood-flash and held out his hand to her.

When they reached the rope ladder, he said, "Hold the light, Sherri, and I'll show you the easiest way to climb."

Taking hold of the ropes on either side of the ladder, he said, "Now instead of stepping on the rung in the usual way, wrap your leg around to the backside of the ladder and hook your heel over the rung. See, like this. Now you try a step or two."

"Josh, I really don't think I can make it all the way up there," Sherri said, her voice quavering.

"Yes, you can," he said sharply, knowing he must make her try.

Sherri drew in her breath, surprised at his harshness, then realized why he was speaking so firmly to her.

"You'll just take each step carefully, as slowly as you want to go. Just make sure your foot is securely placed, and hold on tightly. I'll be right behind you every step."

Sherri bit her lip and handed him the large flashlight. After getting a tight grip on the ladder's sides, she wrapped her right leg around the right-hand rope standard as he'd shown her and hooked her heel over the first rung.

The rope rung sagged as she placed her weight on it, and the ladder began to sway menacingly as soon as she raised her other foot from the floor, but it steadied as Josh grabbed onto it.

"I'll be right behind you now, Sherri," he assured her. "The ladder will move again when we start to climb, but don't let it unnerve you. I'll be just two steps below you. You could reach down and touch me if you needed to, but we want to just keep right on going. Do you understand?"

"Yes, Josh," she answered, clearing her throat to rid her voice of its tremble, and lifting her other foot, she put it around the rope ladder and on the next rung.

As they slowly climbed higher and higher, the light, which he had fastened to his belt, cast garish brightness on the circular walls surrounding them. The ladder moved constantly in jerking, ever larger arcs.

Sherri felt nausea rising within her, and she stopped.

"What's wrong, Sherri?" She felt him gently clasp her ankle.

"I'm feeling really dizzy. I don't think I can go any farther."

"Yes, you can," Josh said sternly. Then with gentleness in his voice, "You'll be okay. Take several deep, slow breaths, and try keeping your eyes closed until we get to the top. We're almost halfway now. I'll guide your foot to each next step with my hand so you won't be afraid of slipping."

"My shoes almost slip off with each step I take. If I lose one of them, I won't have any way to keep my foot on the rung and I'll probably fall." Panic was rising in Sherri's voice as she thought of plummeting to the rock floor below.

"Stop it, Sherri!" Josh said. "I'll be very careful of your shoes and make sure they are firmly on each step we take. Come on, now, let's get going; you'll do fine."

Sooner than she'd dared to hope, he said, "Just one more now, Sherri, and you'll feel the ledge above you. But I want you to keep your eyes closed until I've boosted you over the top."

"All right," she said as she felt his hand place her foot on another sagging rope rung. She repositioned her hands and got ready to reach up to feel the ledge.

A moment later his hand was firmly under her thigh and he said, "Spread both arms straight ahead of you on the floor of the passageway. You'll find a piece of metal imbedded in a crack. Grab hold of it."

"Okay, I've got it!" Sherri said, then felt herself pushed up onto the ledge by his firm, steady shove.

Carefully, she got from her stomach to her knees, then stood to her feet.

In another moment or two, he was beside her with a bright glow of light surrounding them. "There," he said, putting his arm around her shoulder, "that wasn't so bad, was it?"

"I was scared to death," Sherri said with a shaky laugh. "Josh, if you hadn't known what to do, I'd still be down there."

"I've done a lot of cave exploring," Josh answered. "Strange that I'd find a cave under my grandfather's home. Do you suppose he knew it was here? Surely he must have, with it connected to the house the way it is."

"I can't be sure, Josh, but I think he may have. I have some things to show you, a few items I found in the desk."

Then, remembering, she grabbed his arm. "We'd better get out of here so we can get that passage entrance closed. I'll explain later. We really must hurry. It may be too late already. Please."

"Okay," he said, unclipping the light from his belt and shining the beam down the passageway. Taking her hand, he led her back over her original route until they reached the stairway up into the entrance hidden behind the bookshelf wall.

Josh was just swinging the tall unit back against the wall when they heard a voice calling from the main upstairs hallway.

"Miss McElroy, you still here? Miss McElroy!"

Sherri gasped, "Just in time, Josh. We just made it."

"What's wrong?" Josh asked, "and who knows you're here?"

Sherri whispered, "It's your grandfather's lawyer, or so he says. I'll explain later."

Sherri slipped into the big chair behind the desk to hide her torn slacks, as Dodson appeared in the doorway. "Why, Mr. Dodson, I didn't expect you back so soon," she said. "I believe you know Josh Stevens from the service station in Scarborough. By the way, do you happen to know if Arnie Morrow is around?" Sherri's mind was searching for reasons to explain why Josh was here. Saying he had business with Arnie would have to do.

Dodson's face showed glaring suspicion as his gaze shifted from her to Josh and back again.

Ignoring her question, Dodson's eyes narrowed, "I thought you left earlier. Why the delay? I saw your car still here"—he glanced at Josh—"and I wondered if perhaps something was going on that I should know about."

Sherri smiled disarmingly at him. "I've almost decided to stay in this area for a while, Mr. Dodson. It's such a charming region and I have some time off from my employment right now."

"I see," Dodson said, looking warily at them. "What are you doing in Fairbanks' study again? And what is he doing in here?" he added, motioning toward Josh.

"I didn't think Mr. Fairbanks would mind if I came in for another look at this lovely room," Sherri answered, giving him another big smile. Then inquiringly she said, "Are you sure you can't use my assistance with whatever you're here for?"

"No! Ah, no, but thank you for asking." Then more casually, he added, "I'm just checking to see that everything's in order here while Fairbanks is away."

"Oh, I'm sure the Morrows are taking care of things nicely," Sherri said.

Dodson seemed to glare at her a moment before giving her a thin, forced smile, "Well, yes, yes, I suppose. Ah, I must be going. Good-day."

Then unexpectedly, Dodson turned back, and directing a forced charm at Sherri, said smoothly, "If you are to be in the vicinity a while, perhaps I could have the pleasure of your company at dinner one evening. Although Scarborough is small, we do have one rather nice eating establishment."

Completely taken aback, Sherri stammered, "I, I'm sorry, but I expect to be occupied while I'm here."

"Perhaps you'll change your mind," Dodson said as he gave a half bow and turning, left.

"Whew!" Sherri said, slumping into the chair, leaning her head back against the soft leather. "That man gives me the creeps."

"It seems you've picked up an admirer in your short time here," Josh said teasingly, "in addition to me, that is."

"I don't trust that man, Josh," Sherri said, overlooking the compliment. "I'm not sure why. He was here earlier today, too."

"What did he want?"

"I don't know," Sherri answered. "He wouldn't say; he just evaded the issue."

"Well, considering all that's going on around here, I can understand your caution," Josh stated. "Come on, let's see about getting your car fixed. Maybe you should rest while I have a look at it."

"That does sound good," Sherri admitted.

Sherri woke to find Josh had put a cover over her as she slept curled up on her bed. She sat up slowly. She felt better, and the throbbing in her head had diminished. As she pushed away the cover and swung her feet to the floor, Josh tapped lightly on the door.

"Sherri, are you awake?" he called softly.

"Come in. I just woke up."

"You've got more color in your cheeks," he smiled as he looked at her from the open door. "Are you feeling better?"

"I think so," she responded, pushing the hair back from her face. "How long did I sleep?"

"You're asking the wrong man," Josh laughed as he held up an empty wrist. "My watch has been broken for a while now."

"Well, at least you won't need to worry about getting another one," she said, rising and moving toward the dresser to begin brushing her hair. "After you get a look at the watch your grandfather sent you—"

She stopped mid-sentence, brush poised in the air.

"Sherri, what's the matter?"

"Oh, Josh, the watch! The watch and the letter from your grandfather. I had them with me when I went into the secret tunnel. I must have dropped them when I fell."

"It'll be okay," Josh reassured her. "I can go back for them. You couldn't have gone far into the passage."

"No, Josh, you don't understand," she groaned, turning toward him. "The key was in the leather packet with those other things."

"The key?" He looked at her quizzically.

"The key that opens the secret passage behind the bookcase. Now we won't be able to get it open again!"

8

"*O*h, Josh. I've lost all the things your grandfather left for you, and now we'll never get them back." She looked at him helplessly, tears beginning to well in her blue eyes.

"Don't worry," he teased, trying to coax back a smile, " 'Abra-cadabra' worked in *The Arabian Nights*. Maybe it'll work to open our mystery cave, too."

Sherri ignored his joke, crossing to the chaise and sitting, shoulders slumped and head down.

Josh crossed the room and sat beside her. "Hey, there's another possibility, too. I've been in enough caves to know they almost always have more than one entrance. The one under this house is so large it could have several."

"But, Josh," she questioned, looking up at him, "what if there's no other way to get into the tunnel?"

"First things first," Josh answered firmly. "Maybe we don't even need another entrance, or your key either. We know now the bookcase moves out. Maybe we can move it out again, even without the key."

He stood and started for the door, then looked back to where she still sat. "Come on. We'll give it a try right now."

Sherri reached in her pocket for a tissue and blew her nose, then rose to follow him to the study where he was already down on one knee examining the floor and the wall at the edge of the unit of bookshelves.

He turned when she came in. "Doesn't look like there's any kind of latch or locking mechanism, or even evidence of any hinges. Whoever wanted to conceal the cave entrance did an awfully good job of it."

Josh stood up, "It seems as solid as most of the room's furnishings. How in the world did you figure out it opened?"

"The desk. Come here, Josh, let me show you." Pulling out the crucial third drawer, Sherri reached in as she had earlier. Locating the metal button, she pushed it, pulling the drawer to its full extension.

"Look."

Kneeling down and peering in, Josh gave a low whistle, "Well, what do you know! Looks like an extra large keyhole. That takes the key you were talking about?"

"Yes, and when the key is turned, the bookcase moves away from the wall."

"Well, what do you know!" he exclaimed.

"What are we going to do, Josh?"

"First thing we're going to do is leave this for a while," he answered. "Those things in the cave aren't going anywhere, and frankly, I'm hungry, and I'll bet you are, too."

Sherri smiled at him and nodded. "Then let's go get some lunch. We'll figure this out later," he said, letting her walk out first through the study door.

Then closing it behind them, he asked, "Can I help you get your things?"

"Yes, my bag is in my room; my suitcases are still in my car."

———

Later, driving into the outskirts of Scarborough, Josh said, "We'll stop by Mrs. Kirk's, the place where I stay. Although I usually don't eat there on Sundays, she always invites me every week anyway. I'm sure she'll be home by now and will want to meet you."

"Sunday?" Sherri said, "I feel like I've lost track of time."

"No wonder; you've been through some unusual experiences," Josh answered, guiding the red Mustang through the Sunday afternoon quiet of the little town.

"What lovely old trees line this street!" Sherri exclaimed as they neared the edge of a residential area. "I didn't really notice them yesterday. I guess my mind was too involved with other things to take in the beauty. Even without their leaves, they have great dignity, don't they?"

Then she added quietly, "Last evening seems like ages ago; so much has happened."

When they reached the place where she had first seen him, he drove into a gravel drive beside the service station and followed it back to a grove of maple trees.

"Mrs. Kirk had been trying to run this place by herself since her son died last winter, although she pretends it wasn't difficult because she had often helped out. But for a woman her age I imagine it was hard during the harsh cold weather they had here this year. And she didn't have anyone to handle the repairs, so that was a concern for her."

Josh slowed the car as they approached a grove of trees. "When I arrived in town, she needed help and I needed a job and a place to stay."

Josh grinned. "It's worked out well; I'm a fair mechanic and she's a great cook, so it's been good for both of us."

Stopping where the gravel met a flagstone walk leading back through the trees, he got out and came around to Sherri's door. "This is a pretty little spot. Mrs. Kirks' ancestors evidently have had a business of some sort here for a long time, so it has real ties for her. I was fortunate Martha suggested I live here too; she offered me the use of her late son's room as part of my salary."

"It's beautiful," Sherri said, marveling at the wide band of yellow daffodils and blue muscari lining the walk on both sides. Beyond them, Dutchman's-breeches and May apples were pushing up in swaths beneath the leafless trees that were just supporting buds on their limbs.

Just before they reached the cottage, Sherri exclaimed at the beauty of a small pond surrounded by the tightly curled, pale-green fronds of ferns emerging at the base of some young willows.

As they stepped onto the front porch, she noticed the two white wicker rockers plumped with bright yellow cushions, and heavy clay pots of fragrant narcissis beside them.

Josh knocked on the screen door. "Martha," he called. After several moments, a short, smiling woman emerged, pushing a straying wave of graying black hair back behind her ear.

"Well, I see you finally found her, Josh, but I missed you at church. Do come in," she said, holding the door open.

"Sherri, this is Mrs. Kirk," Josh said; "Martha, Sherri McElroy. She's here on some business for Mr. Fairbanks."

"You're very welcome in my home, Sherri," Mrs. Kirk said, her dark eyes smiling gently behind frameless glasses.

Taking Sherri's hand in her soft, plump one, she led her into a comfortable living room.

Then turning to look directly into Sherri's eyes, she said, "You look very worn out. Have you two had dinner?"

"No, we haven't, Martha," Josh answered for both of them. "Sherri had a fall this morning, so I decided she'd be more comfortable here than eating out somewhere. I hoped you wouldn't mind."

"I'm so glad you brought her here, Josh." Mrs. Kirk smiled. "I waited to eat, feeling that you might possibly come. I'll be very pleased to have your company, both of you," she said, smoothing her apron over a flowered dress.

"Now, you just sit down and make yourself right at home," she added, bustling toward the kitchen.

Josh chuckled, "She loves caring for people."

Sherri laughed lightly, "She is a bit like a little mother bird, isn't she?"

She sat down in a brightly flowered chintz armchair and gazed around at the pleasant room. The large braided rug nearly covered the polished wood floor, and an old but well-polished piano stood in one corner. She could smell the faint scent of the red geraniums blooming in white pots on the wide windowsills.

Sherri leaned back against the softness of the chair, relaxing completely, and looked over at Josh where he was settling into a large, worn-looking, brown leather chair. "I suppose that was her husband's," she commented.

"Yes, it was," Mrs. Kirk said, coming through the door with a tall glass of apple juice in each hand. "Sat there reading every evening, he did. Thirty-three years we had together. He was a good man, and I miss him still, though he's been gone some time now."

She handed the crystal glasses to them. "I hope you enjoy apple juice. I bottled this last autumn. I like homemade juice so much better than juice made from concentrate, don't you?"

"Yes, I do," Sherri said, smiling at Mrs. Kirk. "I enjoyed my grandmother's juice when I was a child. If she still visits the orchard, I'll probably have some again soon, as I'll be visiting my grandparents in a few days."

"How fortunate you are to still have living grandparents, Sherri," Mrs. Kirk said. "I never knew mine."

"I didn't either," Sherri heard Josh say quietly.

Mrs. Kirk turned to head for the kitchen, "I'm putting on some chicken to fry," she said, "then I'll be back in a jiffy after I go to the garden for some early lettuce and a few green onions."

"Let us do the garden," Josh said, setting his already half-emptied glass on a small table beside his chair.

"Yes, please," Sherri said, "I haven't been in a vegetable

garden since I was a little girl."

"Well, all right," Mrs. Kirk said, looking pleased. "I'll just peel the potatoes and get the rest of the meal going."

She bustled back into the kitchen, then returning, said, "There's a basket in the kitchen to put the vegetables in, Josh." Turning to Sherri, she asked, "Would you like an apron, dear?"

"No thanks," Sherri answered.

Mrs. Kirk patted Sherri's arm and, smiling, went to the kitchen.

Finishing their juice, Josh and Sherri entered the immaculate kitchen. The aroma of the browning chicken, already beginning to crackle in a big iron skillet, filled the room.

"Smells great," Josh said appreciatively. "Sherri will know why I say you are a great cook after she's tasted that." He reached over and took a small brown basket from its peg on the wall.

"I'm glad you enjoy the food here, Josh," Mrs. Kirk said as she stood at the sink, peeling potatoes.

Then she moved to the stove and picked up a long-tined fork as Sherri and Josh stepped out the door and into the tidy backyard.

"Josh, just look at all the pretty flowers," Sherri said, indicating at the masses of early tulips growing around the perimeter of lawn.

"Yes, it's great, Sherri. Mrs. Kirk has everything looking so nice."

Josh sauntered over to an arbor that formed an entrance through a low, white picket fence surrounding the garden area.

"Better stay there and admire the flowers, Sherri," he said from the other side of the fence. "Looks like the storm last night has turned this soil into mud in most places."

"All right." Sherri turned to watch a robin hopping

across the still-wet grass in search of a delicacy..

She walked back toward the house and sat on a bench in an alcove near the door.

Josh joined her in a few minutes, putting the little brown basket between them on the bench where she could see the bunches of curled green lettuce leaves and smell the pungency of the slim white onions. Sherri took a deep sniff then quicky closed her eyes, her hand to her head.

"Sherri, are you feeling okay?"

"Just a little dizzy. I'll be all right."

Reaching out his hand, he took hers in a firm clasp, helping her to rise.

Mrs. Kirk turned from the sink with a smile when they entered. "I'll clean the lettuce and onions, Martha," Josh said, "while you and Sherri get acquainted."

"Why, thank you, Josh," Mrs. Kirk said as she walked over to the stove and adjusted the flame under the pan of potatoes.

"Just give me a minute to turn these chicken pieces and I'll be right with you, dear," she added, smiling at Sherri. "You go in and sit down."

In the living room, Sherri sank gratefully into the armchair, glad for a few minutes alone. She laid her head back and closed her eyes.

"Sherri," Josh called softly.

He was standing beside her when she opened her eyes. "Yes?"

"Dinner's ready."

"It's ready? So soon?"

"You've been sleeping," Josh grinned.

"Oh," Sherri said, taking the offered hand, "Mrs. Kirk must think I'm terribly rude."

"Not at all. I told her that when you fell you hit your head, and that you didn't sleep well last night. By the way, I think you ought to let a doctor check you over."

"I do, too," Mrs. Kirk said as they entered the kitchen. "Doc McDaniel lives not far from here, and he hinted after church that he hasn't had any of my chocolate cake for a while." She smiled mischievously, "I told him to come for coffee late this afternoon, because I baked one yesterday."

She came over to Sherri and put her hand on her arm, "We'll just have him take a look at you while he's here. He won't mind at all."

After patting her gently, Mrs. Kirk put a large pitcher of milk on the table, then a bowl of carrots and one of creamy whipped potatoes. "I'll just give him a call after we've eaten and tell him to bring his bag along."

"Thank you, Mrs. Kirk," Sherri said as Josh pulled out her chair. "I suppose it would be a good idea if you're sure he won't feel imposed upon."

"I know he won't. He's a dear man. Best friend of my husband, he was. He's enjoyed many of my chocolate cakes on Sunday afternoons."

Removing her apron, Mrs. Kirk settled her ample self in a chair opposite Sherri at the big round table.

"Now, Josh, you may get the platter of chicken from the warming oven, and the biscuits, too."

After he was seated, she smiled contentedly at them both, "How very nice it is to have young people at the table again." Then bowing her head, "Josh, will you please ask our heavenly Father's blessing on us and this food?"

As they enjoyed the crisp salad and hot biscuits, Sherri listened to Mrs. Kirk's recounting of the morning church service and brief highlights of the sermon.

"After the service," Mrs. Kirk continued, "Rev. Wolford asked if I'd heard anything from Joshua Fairbanks, but I haven't, of course." Mrs. Kirk looked questioningly from Josh to Sherri.

"Mr. Fairbanks has been ill," Sherri said quietly.

"Oh, dear," Mrs. Kirk said, deep concern evident in

her eyes. "You know, he took to coming here occasionally and talking with my husband. Many years ago that was, after his wife died. He seemed awfully lonely. They had first met down by the river, my husband and Joshua, where they were both fishing."

Mrs. Kirk wasn't looking at either of the young people; her glance had strayed to the window, seemingly lost in memories as she spoke. Then she smiled at Sherri, "He's been here real often in more recent years, until my Peter died, that is. He's a right friendly man, Mr. Fairbanks is, though he does seem very quiet in most ways. Never cared to talk about his family."

After a short pause, Mrs. Kirk continued, "I haven't seen him since shortly after my son's funeral. He stopped by to ask if there was something he could do, or anything I needed. Said he was going to be away for a while."

Mrs. Kirk had risen and was removing the salad plates. While she was gone, Josh reached over and touched Sherri's arm, "Would you mind if I told Martha exactly why you're here? I think it might be best to confide in her."

"Why, of course not," Sherri answered. "It's really more your business than mine, anyway, Josh."

Returning to the table, Mrs. Kirk passed the platter of chicken to Sherri, saying, "Josh, you start the vegetables, will you?"

While they ate, Mrs. Kirk and Josh chatted about plans for the vegetable garden, with Sherri joining in to comment admiringly on the beautiful flowers in the yard.

It was when the slices of peach pie were being served that Josh said, "Martha, I have something very serious to tell you. It concerns Mr. Fairbanks."

"Yes?" Mrs. Kirk lifted the coffee carafe and filled Sherri's cup, then his.

"Martha, Mr. Fairbanks is my grandfather."

"Your grandfather!" she exclaimed. "Well, I declare."

Then, filling her own cup and passing the cream pitcher, she asked, "But why haven't you told me before? Did he know you were coming?"

"I arrived earlier than he expected. That's why he wasn't here when I came to town," Josh said.

"Well, that won't matter once he gets back. It'll be a nice surprise for him."

Josh said quietly, "He won't be back. He died a few days ago."

"Died?" A look of dismay crossed her face, "What happened?"

"A massive heart attack," Sherri answered. "He died in New York, and was buried there."

"Oh my, that poor man. And all alone he was," Mrs. Kirk said, her eyes filling with tears.

"Not exactly, Martha; Sherri's been with him. She was his nurse."

Mrs. Kirk reached over and patted Sherri's arm, "A nurse you are. That's fine. I'm glad you were with him. Such a fine gentleman, so dignified."

Turning to Josh, she said, "You're probably the only family he had. I'm so sorry you didn't get to see him before he died."

"I am, too." Josh looked away for a moment. "But he'd made arrangements for Sherri to meet me and deliver a message from him. That's been a comfort, to know he cared about me."

"Well," said Mrs. Kirk, "it's sad news, even though he was getting on in years. But he loved the Lord very much; talked often about Him, he did."

Then she brightened, smiling at Sherri, "Speaking of messages, if you're feeling well enough, I do hope you'll attend our little church with us this evening."

"Thank you, Mrs. Kirk, that would be nice. I'd like that."

Following dinner, Sherri was sent to take a nap while Josh brought her luggage in from the car.

———

The sun was low in the western sky when Sherri awoke. Except for a dull ache on one side of her head, she felt much better than she had. Sitting on the edge of the bed in Mrs. Kirk's serene bedroom, Sherri stretched, yawning, and discovered she had extremely sore shoulder and arm muscles. When she stood, she realized that her thighs ached, also.

Must be from my tenseness on the rope ladder, she thought, remembering the fear with which she had made the climb. A great sense of thankfulness for their safety flowed over her. "Thank you, God," she said softly. "Thank you."

Sherri went into the bathroom, delighted to find an old-fashioned claw-footed tub, complete with a wire soap dish hanging on its high curved rim. A bath would be wonderful!

Sherri soaked in the luxury of the tub, enjoying the picture the begonia plant on the windowsill made, spilling its mass of pink blossoms out between the ruffles of the white lace tieback curtains. "This place is so much like my grandparents'," she mused as she dried herself with a fluffy, lavendar-scented towel. Perhaps that was why she felt so at home here.

Back in the bedroom, she brushed her hair and tied it back in a ponytail. Then she put on a long, slim jean skirt, a casual white blouse, and slipped into a pair of brown leather sandals.

John McDaniel arrived at the door at exactly 5:30. He was a distinguished-looking gentleman in a gray suit and charcoal tie.

He handed a small ribbon-tied box of bonbons to Mrs. Kirk as he removed his gray fedora, revealing abundant white hair around a bald spot.

As Sherri had just entered the room, Mrs. Kirk said,

"John, this is Miss McElroy, a friend of Josh's."

Turning, she added, smiling, "Sherri, this is Dr. McDaniel."

Sherri stepped forward as he moved toward her, and she found her hand clasped in a strong, firm grasp, friendly hazel eyes mirroring the same sincerity expressed by the man's generous smile.

"I'm delighted to meet you, Miss McElroy. It's a pleasure to have the company of two lovely ladies this evening," he said gallantly.

In addition to the chocolate-iced chocolate cake, Mrs. Kirk had set the table with a platter of sliced cold chicken and ham, a chunky loaf of home-baked rye bread, and a bowl of her homemade pickles. The coffee was already perking and a tall pitcher of milk was on a lace doily next to the cream and sugar.

During the pleasant mealtime and easy small talk, Sherri realized how much she missed this cozy sense of being with such comfortable people. She felt so secure, like being with family.

Dr. McDaniel had pushed away from the table following his second slice of cake. "Martha, you certainly have no contenders in baking," he said. Giving Josh a friendly wink, he added, "She surely knows the way to a man's heart, doesn't she, lad?"

Then he turned to Sherri, "I understand you had a bit of an accident. As soon as you like, I'll check you."

As Sherri nodded assent, he said, "Shall we step into the living room? I left my bag near the front door." Then, to put her at ease, he added with a nice smile, "After that, I believe I have the pleasure of accompanying you folks to church."

———

Swept clear of clouds by the winds of the night before,

the sky above them sparkled with numberless stars as they walked the few blocks to the old stone church.

The light through the stained-glass windows glowed a welcome as they arrived, and Sherri felt more at ease than she had in a long time as she was introduced to several of the other worshipers.

She found herself enjoying the vibrant singing of the congregation.

Settled cozily in between Josh and Mrs. Kirk, Sherri sighed and let her thoughts begin to drift. But she tuned back into the church service when she heard the elderly minister say, "Our text tonight is from the book of Job."

Job? Wasn't the Bible reference scratched on Mr. Fairbanks' watch from the book of Job? Perhaps the pastor's thoughts would give some insight on why that reference was so important to Josh's grandfather. Sherri sat up to listen.

"Job knew what it was like to hurt," Rev. Walford began, peering over the top of his glasses. He went on to tell the story of how, in one day, Job lost everything—his children, his wealth, his health.

Moving to the side of the pulpit, he leaned against it. "From all appearances, the things that happened to Job were completely unjust and senseless, because he had been a righteous man all his life."

Sherri straightened a bit. It was as if the minister had overheard her conversation with Josh the night before. Like Job, she knew how it felt to lose those dearest to her. But she had never considered that Job might have wrestled with the unjustice of his losses. She leaned forward in her seat, listening closely now.

The white-haired gentleman went on. "As his friends confused him, and the pain of his losses pressed in, there were surely times when Job was unsure about what he believed. Yet he found peace."

Stepping back, he lifted the Bible in his hands. "Let me

read Job 19:25. Even when Job didn't understand God's ways, he said this, 'I know that my Redeemer lives. . . .' He experienced the reality of God's presence because he chose to believe in God's goodness, even in the face of tragedy. With God's help, he could find strength. He could know peace, even in sorrow. Though he had lost everything, he was not alone."

Not alone. Sherri's mind flashed back to that morning in the cave when she had cried out with a desperate prayer. Even though Josh hadn't appeared at that moment, she remembered the sense of a quieting Presence with her, calming her panic and subduing her terror. Was that the peace Job experienced? If it was, how could she find it as she still struggled with the death of her parents?

Walking back to Mrs. Kirk's with her and Josh, Sherri's mind was full of what she had heard. She was so immersed in her thoughts that Mrs. Kirk had to speak twice before Sherri heard her.

"Since the doctor said he felt you'd be all right after a good rest, dear, I hope you'll consider spending the night with me. I have an extra bed in my room where you can be comfortable, and I'll be nearby in case you should get to feeling poorly."

"Oh, thank you, Mrs. Kirk," Sherri answered, "that's a relief. I really wasn't sure what I was going to do."

"All right, then, that's all settled. The three of us will have some hot chocolate and go to bed early."

"That sounds good to me," Josh said. "I want to get up early tomorrow so I can get back to Grandfather's house for an hour or so before I open the station."

Mrs. Kirk stopped him. "You're to take tomorrow off, Josh, so you and Sherri can take care of whatever it is you find necessary to do. I've serviced cars many times over the years, and there is nothing extra to be done for several days, nothing at all this week, actually, so I can handle it fine until someone needs repairs."

––––––––––

The sun was shining brightly through the filmy curtain when Sherri awoke the next morning. She could hear Mrs. Kirk working in the kitchen even before she rolled over and saw her empty bed.

The aroma of bacon and coffee wafted into the room while Sherri changed from her nightgown into a pair of jeans and a soft, worn sweatshirt.

After breakfast, as Josh was holding the car door for her, he asked, "Are you sure you feel all right today? I could search for another entrance to the cave by myself, you know."

"I feel fine, honestly. Besides, I want to be there. It's my fault your things are lost. And I wouldn't want to miss the excitement of this search anyway. I'm looking forward to continuing it."

"Good. But there's bound to be a lot of walking, and you probably shouldn't push yourself too hard yet."

"I won't, Josh. I'll stop if I start having problems. Fortunately, I had these old tennis shoes in my suitcase, so the walking shouldn't be any problem."

They walked the grounds for hours, searching for likely spots to check, anything Josh thought might possibly conceal an opening.

"We're not looking for something large, anything obvious," Josh had told her. "Often the openings are very small, too small for a person to enter. Sometimes they have gotten covered with undergrowth or hidden by some change in the land, manmade or otherwise."

Late in the morning, discouraged, they went into the mansion, and finding none of the Morrows around, made a quick lunch from the coffee cake and a couple of apples.

"Let's see if there's a basement, Sherri. That would be a logical place for another way into the cave."

"Good idea, Josh. I was wondering about that."

The area extending below part of the house proved to be more of an earth-floored cellar than a regular basement.

Its low ceiling of heavy cross-timbers was draped with dusty cobwebs. Josh pushed them aside as they entered the musty, darkened room, his flashlight probing into the corners and behind ceiling-high shelves of crocks and empty fruit jars.

"Josh, look!" Sherri exclaimed, pointing toward a low, narrow door at the far end of the room.

"Maybe that's it!"

9

*W*hen they reached the three-foot-high door, they found it had strong iron hinges and seemed to be locked.

Testing its sturdiness, Josh said, "I'll check around and see if I can find something to force this open."

Turning to Sherri, he asked, "Do you want to wait here? I have that small extra flashlight in my jacket pocket."

"All right," Sherri said, taking the light from him and flicking it on.

It didn't seem long at all until she heard returning footsteps and turned to go meet Josh where the room made a jog into another larger one.

But it wasn't Josh who met her smile of greeting.

Instead, she was confronted by a burly, completely bald, unshaven man dressed in soiled overalls, carrying a big flashlight and a large pipewrench.

Seemingly as startled as she was, he stepped back, "Who are you? What are you doing here?" His almost colorless eyes quickly scanned her face, then darted searchingly around the dim room.

Before she had time to answer, she saw Josh behind the man. The fellow had heard him, and whirling, temporarily blinded Josh with his light.

"What's going on here? Who are you two?" he demanded, his voice impatient and harsh.

"Get that light out of my eyes," Josh said. "We're not here to harm anything. Anyway, who are you?"

As the short, stocky man lowered his muscular arm, he muttered, "I'm the caretaker here." Then as Josh approached, the man eyed him. "Haven't I seen you over to Mrs. Kirk's place?"

"Yes, Josh Stevens," he said, extending his hand. "I'm Joshua Fairbanks' grandson, and this is Sherri McElroy, a friend of his."

"Ya don't say," Morrow said, ignoring Josh's outstretched hand and looking as though he wasn't sure whether to believe him or not. "Well, what'd you want down here?"

"Sort of checking the place over. I'm sure you're doing a good job with everything around the place, but I've never visited here before, so I'm interested in how the house is built."

Changing the subject, Morrow asked, "How'd ya get in? Fairbanks isn't here."

Sherri spoke up, "Oh, Mr. Fairbanks gave me a key. He sent me here to take care of some things for him." She felt nervous and hoped she wasn't saying too much.

"I see. Well, Stevens, did you want to see anything in particular?"

"I was wondering about this old door," Josh answered. "What's behind it, more food storage area?"

"Naw, leads to some of the plumbing. That's where I was going now. Usually take a couple of wrenches and check everything out once a year. Never can tell about these old pipes, though they seem sound enough."

"Mind if I take a look with you?" Josh asked

"Nope, c'mon along. Pretty dirty in there, though," he answered, selecting a key from a large ring he'd taken from one of his bulging pockets.

Before following him, Josh dusted off a crate that was propped against the wall nearby, "Here, Sherri, have a seat. I won't be long."

Later, as Morrow stooped to follow Josh back through the small doorway, he said, "Didn't know Fairbanks had a grandson. You must be 'bout the same age as my son, Arnie."

"We've met at the station several times," Josh answered, as the three of them headed together to the stairs that led up into the kitchen.

"I live in another part of the country and had never made a trip here before," Josh said to Ross Morrow, "and I thought it was about time I did."

Sherri could tell that Josh, too, felt suspicious of this man.

After Morrow had left, Josh said, "I didn't want to be too obvious in searching around. Besides, he seemed to be watching me as much as he was checking the pipes that ran through there."

"Do you think he wasn't telling the truth?" Sherri asked.

"I don't know," Josh answered thoughtfully.

Going into the kitchen, Sherri asked, "Would you like me to make some coffee?"

After Josh shook his head, she added, "I didn't think to ask Mr. Morrow about his wife. Do you feel we ought to?"

"Better just let it ride for a day or so. There are too many loose ends here," Josh said. "He surely wouldn't be following his usual work routine if his wife were missing or injured. But also, I don't want to make the wrong person suspicious of us," he added, "not only about what we're doing, but about your seeing the dead woman."

"Then you believe I really saw a body?"

"It's conceivable."

"Conceivable! Honestly, Josh, you make me almost angry at you!" Then calming, Sherri said, "Actually, I'm torn between being upset at your questioning what I'm sure was true, and my respect for your clear thinking."

"I'd listen to the part of you that respects me," he answered teasingly, giving her a quick grin.

Sherri rolled her eyes upward as though she were having to deal with a misbehaving child, and she too, laughed.

"Seriously, Josh, there's something I'd like to show you on the desk in the study. Could we do that now?"

"Sure. Come on."

As they walked through the intervening rooms to the foyer and up the stairs, Sherri told him about the watch that had belonged to his great-great-grandfather and its inscribed numbers and letters.

She explained how she had searched the desk and eventually figured out the meaning of the letter-number combination.

"You've got a quick mind, Sherri. I'm proud of you," Josh said as they reached the top of the stairs.

Turning to thank him, she saw the admiration in his eyes, and something else that caused her heart to skip a beat.

She turned back quickly. "The carving on this door matches the design on the watch," she said, pointing to the door of her room as they passed it. "I'm sure it's not a coincidence."

Continuing to the study, Sherri approached the spacious desk, its dark wood mellow in the light from the tall window behind it.

"I want you to look at the photo and its frame," Sherri said. Walking behind the desk, Josh sat in the large leather chair and picked up the small oval frame.

"Wonder who she is?"

"I thought it was perhaps your grandmother when she was young."

"Yes, I suppose so."

"Turn it over, Josh. Look at it carefully."

"Hmmm. Looks like DR–R–3."

"Yes, and as I discovered, it refers to that third desk drawer." Sherri bent and opened it a crack.

"Ingenious. I wonder who designed it?"

"Evidently one of your ancestors."

"Pretty clever person, whoever he was," Josh answered.

"You may be interested in looking through the desk. There seem to be family mementoes in some of the drawers. Oh, and in the third drawer, there's your grandfather's journal. You'll be so glad to read it. He mentions you, and your father, too."

Josh opened the drawer and pulled out the slim volume. Sherri knew he'd want a few quiet moments as he read, so she turned her attention to the bookshelves across the room.

A few minutes later, Sherri called him to join her. She was looking at a framed photo of a young woman leaning against the trunk of a tree, its leafy branches spreading above her head.

"What is it, Sherri?" he asked as she removed the photo from where it stood between a group of slim books of poetry and a set of Byron.

"Doesn't this look familiar?"

Taking it from her, Josh said, "She does resemble the girl in the desk photo."

"No, I mean the tree. Didn't we see some like it today?"

"You're right, Sherri," he said, walking over to the window. "I believe it's a walnut. I noticed some when we were near the pasture area. They were over toward the small grove of pines near the hill."

As Josh lifted the picture closer, examining the face of the woman, Sherri said, "Josh, look at the outer edge of the frame, just below your left thumb."

"Well, I'll be! It's the same DR-R-3, plus what looks like Job 38:22."

"The watch had a Bible reference from Job, too," Sherri said, "but I don't recall what it was."

"Let's check and see what it says," Josh said, reaching for a large Bible lying on a small table nearby.

Josh sat back down at the desk and opening the book's worn leather cover, thumbed carefully through the fragile pages.

"Here it is, the twenty-second verse of Job thirty-eight; 'Hast thou entered into the treasures of the snow? Or hast thou seen the treasures of the hail,' " Josh paused, then looked up, "The next verse says, 'which I have reserved against the time of trouble?' Then there's more along that same line."

"What do you think it means?" Sherri asked.

"Well, the next few verses explain what the writer meant, but I haven't the slightest idea what the person who inscribed the watch and frame intended it to mean."

"The verses talk about treasure, treasure 'reserved against the time of trouble.' Do you suppose there's a family treasure, Josh?"

"I guess that's always a possibility," Josh admitted. "But the verse says it's a treasure of the snow. What does snow have to do with something valuable?"

With a puzzled expression on her face, Sherri asked, "Since the Scripture reference was on the watch with the DR–R–3, and the DR–R–3 led me to the opening of the tunnel entrance, do you suppose the inscription on this frame has a connection to the same area, that maybe the tree is in some way involved?"

"You may have something there," Josh answered. "The same question has been running through my mind."

Opening a desk drawer, he removed a pencil and a sheet of paper. He made a quick sketch of the tree, then folded the paper and put it in his shirt pocket. Getting up and pushing the chair back against the desk, he walked over to the bookshelves and replaced the framed picture.

"Want to join me in trying to locate this old walnut?"

"Yes," Sherri answered, excitement in her voice, joining him as he went out the door, shutting it firmly behind them.

Downstairs in the foyer, Josh said, "There's a spot nearby we didn't cover this morning. I discovered a walled garden the other night. I had forgotten about it until just now. Want to check it out first on our way to the walnut grove?"

"Yes, let's go," she said, following him through the dining room and down the long hall.

Evergreen ivy grew over most of the eight-foot-high wall and the side of the house that it joined. Moss was heavy at its base.

Dense patches of pale pink and yellow tulips filled an area where the sun was beginning to warm a pair of ancient iron benches half-hidden by a mass of wisteria vines clambering over them.

An abundance of ferns were unfolding in this secluded sanctuary, and Sherri delighted at the beauty of a flowering tree behind the benches.

"This must have been a favorite spot of your grandmother's," she said, bending to remove a broken branch and several handfuls of old leaves from a tiny pool constructed of small, smooth stones.

"Yes, I suppose it was," Josh answered from where he was pushing aside the thick growth of vines to probe the lower portions of the wall.

After searching the perimeter thoroughly and finding nothing that seemed promising, Sherri unlatched the sturdy cedar door in the wall, and they went out into the landscaped area beyond.

Passing through what had once been well-kept gardens, they came to the boarded-up stable at the edge of a large overgrown pasture.

"See the tree over there, Sherri," Josh said, pointing,

"beyond the far edge of the pasture and to the right?"

"Yes, those trees do look somewhat like the tree in the picture, but I'm not sure."

"Want to hike over there and check them out? They're going to have a different appearance, all of them, because the one in the photo was partially in leaf," Josh said. "But the one we want will have the same limbs as the one in the photo."

Reaching for the hand he offered, Sherri said, "How did you recognize the tree in the picture as a walnut, anyway? To me, a tree is a tree."

"The summer I was eleven, an elderly neighbor who loved the outdoors taught me how to tell one tree type from another. Never thought I'd be using it like this!"

As they neared the stand of trees, she said, "None of them look like a twin of the picture, do they?"

"That'll be difficult to determine until we check each one from different angles, because we have no idea from what location the picture was snapped. Also, if that was my grandmother, or perhaps my great-grandmother, in the picture, the tree will have grown a lot since then. That means, too, that we can eliminate the obviously younger trees from the old ones."

"Of course. I didn't think of that."

"Now, notice on this sketch I made," Josh said. "See the unusual amount of space between these two branches on this side. It's as though one or more is missing."

Refolding the paper and putting it back in his pocket, he continued, "We'll just walk around each tree, at a bit of a distance, and see if one resembles this branching. You can go that direction if you like, and I'll check over this way. It'll save us some time."

Sherri returned dejected when they met after their separate walks. "No luck. I felt so sure we'd find it."

"Don't be discouraged, Sherri," he consoled her.

"That frame may have had another picture in it originally. It's possible that the photo and the inscription have no connection. We have a hidden cave opening on our minds, so it was easy to jump to conclusions about what might be a clue."

"Yes, I guess you're right," she said.

Then she smiled, "There's a large patch of forsythia bushes beyond that hill. I saw them when I was over that way looking at one of the trees. Would you mind cutting some for Mrs. Kirk? They are so bright and cheerful, and I didn't notice any in her yard."

"Sure thing," Josh said, starting in that direction at a jog. "You wait. It'll only take a few minutes."

Sherri sank down on a nearby rock and began picking off burrs that had clung to her jeans. "I look like a porcupine," she laughed to herself. "This field seems to have burrs scattered all over, especially these short, spiny ones."

She sat quietly then, absorbed in warm thoughts of Josh. It was difficult to realize that a few days ago she hadn't known he existed. It was such fun to be with him.

The sun was warm, and Sherri began to drowse.

She started as a pair of birds alighted nearby and began busily searching for weed seeds. She realized then that Josh had been gone much longer than a few minutes.

For no reason that she could pinpoint, her heart began to beat faster with a strange fear.

Getting up quickly from the rock, she ran in the direction where Josh had disappeared earlier around the curve of the overgrown hill.

As she passed the forsythia bushes, she saw him. He was kneeling near an outcrop of rock just at the base of the hill, half-hidden by the trunk of a large tree.

Her gaze followed the upward surge of the massive tree trunk to a spot where there was a large open space, a space as though some branches were missing. Josh had found the tree!

10

Hurrying over to him, Sherri asked excitedly, "Is this it, Josh? Is this really the tree in the photo?"

"It looked enough like it, Sherri, for me to want to come check it out."

"What are you doing?" she asked, watching him moving brush and football-size stones into a pile.

"There's an opening of some sort here, but it's clogged with debris."

"Then you may have found it! Do you think you've finally found another way into the cave?"

"Could be, but don't get your hopes up. It's likely an animal den of some sort."

"Oh," Sherri said disappointedly. "Can I help you?"

"No thanks. I put Mrs. Kirk's blossoms over there," he said, waving in the general direction.

She saw the flowers, then, impatient for a better look at the opening he'd found, she climbed up onto the large rock above where he worked. "Josh, there is a house beyond those pines. Several other small buildings, too. Do you suppose that's where the Morrows live?"

"Possibly. Their home is somewhere on this property."

He got up from his knees, brushing off his jeans. Scrambling down from the rock, Sherri saw the opening he had cleared. It was approximately three feet wide and two feet high. Even now, it was still partially hidden by the branches of several small overhanging bushes and some other taller ones standing about five feet in front of it.

"How did you ever see it, Josh, especially with all that stuff over it?"

"I noticed the tree while I was cutting the branches of forsythia for Mrs. Kirk. That lack of branches on the tree's one side was so like the picture, I knew I had to check the area now or wonder about it all night."

Dropping to one knee, he said, "Come take a look inside."

Crouching beside him, Sherri strained to see the interior, but except for the packed soil area just inside, she could make out nothing but some rocks strewn about. It was so dark she could barely see the walls of the cave and could not determine its size.

"Do you really believe it's an animal's den, Josh?"

"No, not now, if it ever was. I was able to tell better after clearing the opening. At least I don't think it's been used recently, unless maybe for a temporary shelter from a storm or a predator. There's usually an animal odor when it's occupied. There may be a few bats farther in if the cavity extends for any distance, but I haven't noticed any signs."

"So it could possibly lead to the cave we were in?"

"If it isn't confined to just one small area here," Josh said, "it very well may connect somewhere. But it's too late today to explore it. Besides, if it turns out to be more than just a short tunnel, I don't have adequate equipment with me."

Sherri picked up the forsythia branches as Josh said, "There are some things in Martha's garage I can use to put together caving equipment. I'll drop you off at her place, then see if I can get some extra items in town, just in case I may need them."

"While you're gone, I'll try again to get my grandparents on the phone, to let them know I'll be delayed. The storm evidently took down some lines and I couldn't reach them yesterday. I told Mrs. Kirk that they wouldn't be worried about me yet, because I had planned to stay with a girlfriend on the way and wouldn't have arrived at their home until this afternoon."

Mrs. Kirk was delighted with the forsythia and immediately put them in water in a tall, narrow-topped crock that stood in a corner of her kitchen.

"This was the bottom of our butter churn," she said with a smile, "but we haven't kept cows for many years. Every spring since, I've used this for forcing branches to bud. Always he brought them to me, my husband did. And then afterward, my son."

She wiped tears from her eyes with the hem of her large white apron. "Sure, and I didn't expect to have any this year, but you've brought some already in bloom. You're a very thoughtful girl, Sherri. I appreciate these more than you can possibly imagine."

"I enjoyed doing it," Sherri responded, giving her a warm hug. "From the appearance of your yard, I knew you loved flowers. Actually, Josh cut them for you."

Mrs. Kirk patted Sherri's arm, "Well, you are both fine young people. I wish you could have known Peter Junior. You'd have made fine friends for him."

"And now," she added briskly, moving to the stove for the teakettle, "how would you like to join me for a cup of tea before I start supper?"

"That sounds very nice."

———

When Josh arrived, slices of beef and onion were simmering in an aromatic sauce of tomatoes and herbs.

Sherri looked up from the bowl where she was tossing a salad. "Did you get the items you needed?"

"I can make do with what I've found. Boy, whatever you're cooking, it sure smells great."

"It'll be ready soon," Mrs. Kirk said, testing the potatoes baking in the oven. "The newspaper is in its usual place by Peter's chair."

Mrs. Kirk bustled over to the table and began arranging china and flatware. "I think it's good for Josh having you here, Sherri. I didn't feel he got out enough. Almost all the time he was either working in the station and garage or in his room studying from the pile of books he keeps there."

She put butter and honey on the table. "I suggested he go out some evenings, that I would tend the station, but he always declined. Said he had studying to do and things to figure out about his life. I didn't pry and ask what things, but I've been praying that God will guide him in whatever the decisions are."

Then Mrs. Kirk poured milk into tall glasses. "Peter Junior was never fond of books, although he did well enough in school. It was machines that had his attention; he enjoyed so much working on cars, appliances, anything. And good he was, too," she said fondly, the lines of her face softening.

During supper, Josh said, "Martha, I'm going to the garage after I've finished eating and see if I can complete the overhaul on Simpson's car. I know it's not due until the end of the week, but I'd like to have another day or two off if you feel you can manage."

"Of course. And I know the Simpsons will be happy to have their car done early. Their son is interested in that type of work, but he's not quite adept enough right now to do it quickly."

"I'm wondering, too," Josh said, "if Sherri could continue staying here a while."

Before Sherri could say anything, Mrs. Kirk answered, "I would be so glad if she would. Fine company she is. I was never blessed with a daughter, so this is a nice experience for me."

"Good," Josh said with a satisfied smile, looking at

Sherri, his look begging her not to object.

After finishing off a piece of Sunday's cake, he pushed back his chair and excused himself. "If you ladies can get along without my presence," he said with a mischievous grin, "I'll get started with my work. Probably be getting in late, but I'll try not to disturb you."

After they had straightened the kitchen and were sitting in the living room, Sherri said, "Mrs. Kirk, if I stay here, I want to pay you for my room and board."

"No, Sherri, I want you to be my guest," Mrs. Kirk answered, looking up from her knitting.

"But I will really feel better about it if I can repay you in some way."

"All right, dear, I understand. Do you know how to knit or quilt?"

"Yes, I've knitted sweaters and several afghans."

"Good. The women of the church are preparing baby bedcovers for an orphanage. Would you care to make one?"

"Oh, yes. I'll go for yarn tomorrow."

"No need to do that. I have plenty extra," Mrs. Kirk said, rising. "Come pick out the colors you want."

Sherri followed Mrs. Kirk into a small room where a sewing machine stood uncovered next to the floor lamp she had switched on. An old, round, oak dining table was covered by items in various stages of completion. Beneath the ruffled yellow curtains of a wide, low window stood a baby's cradle of dark pine filled with stuffed animals and partially dressed dolls.

Mrs. Kirk had seated herself in a yellow cushioned rocker at the opposite side of the little workroom and opened the top of an old humpback trunk. She lifted out a tray overflowing with old lace doilies, revealing piles of pastel yarns.

Sherri went over and reached into the soft, downy

mass, picking out several skeins of muted yellow and one of white.

"There is a pair of knitting needles standing in the vase on the table," Mrs. Kirk said. "That size works well on this yarn."

Later, sitting comfortably in the living room with the soft balls of yarn in her lap, Sherri began working a quick, simple pattern her mother had taught her years before.

"Did you enjoy our church service last evening, dear?" Mrs. Kirk asked.

"Yes, I did," Sherri answered. "Rev. Wolford seems to be a very sincere man."

"He is. He tries to get us to view our spiritual lives from angles we may not have thought much about before."

"Well, he certainly accomplished that last night," Sherri said. "With me, at least."

"And how was that?" Mrs. Kirk asked, pausing in her knitting.

"Oh, that business about Job losing everything and complaining about the injustice of it all. I'd never realized before someone in the Bible experienced the same feelings I've had."

"You've felt like you've lost everything?" Mrs. Kirk asked.

"Everything that mattered," Sherri sighed. "Both my parents were killed in a car accident six years ago. And I guess I felt angry at the injustice of their deaths. Mrs. Kirk, they were wonderful people! And I needed them so much. Why did they have to die?"

Mrs. Kirk stopped knitting, quieting her hands on the yarn in her lap. She leaned slightly forward in the small overstuffed chair. "Sherri, do you know the Lord as your Savior? Are you sure you're His child?"

"Oh, yes!" Sherri affirmed. "I asked Jesus to come into my life when I was thirteen. But I've grown away from Him since my parents' deaths. I guess I began to wonder if He even cared about me."

Mrs. Kirk picked the knitting up from her lap, her plump fingers manipulating the needles back and forth through the yarn as she waited for Sherri to continue.

"You must have felt those things, Mrs. Kirk. You lost your husband, now your son. You *must* have felt anger at being left alone."

Martha Kirk looked away. "I've known pain all right. When my husband died, I thought my world would end. And losing Peter Junior was losing a part of me. I still cry sometimes when I think of them." Her voice trembled, and she paused, then looked into Sherri's eyes.

"One thing, though. I did lose them, but I've never, never been alone. Even in the darkest times of grief, the Lord has given me His peace and strength. In fact, those are the times when He has been the closest." She was smiling gently now, the peace of which she spoke evident on her face.

Sherri leaned back, sighing. "But didn't you ever wonder why they had to die?"

Reaching down for another skein of blue yarn from the willow basket next to her chair, Mrs. Kirk replied, "I've wondered, of course, how it all fits into God's plan. And I look forward to the day when I'll see it all clearly. But this I do know," she continued, her eyes shining, "I know God is good. Everything He allows is for my best."

"How do you know that?" Sherri insisted.

"Oh, my dear," Mrs. Kirk laughed gently, "I know because He says so in His Word, and I believe Him. And I know because of all the promises He's kept to me these fifty-odd years."

"And, Sherri," she said softly, looking lovingly at the young girl seated across from her, "you can know His kindness, too. He wants to show His love to you, but He can't while you push Him away."

The words of truth should have stung Sherri, but she could sense the love and motherly concern motivating them.

Mrs. Kirk stood up. "Excuse me a moment, Sherri, while I put on water for tea."

As she walked toward the kitchen, Sherri stopped her. "Mrs. Kirk?"

"Yes, dear," she said, turning toward Sherri.

"Thank you for what you said. It's been a long time since I've felt comfortable enough to share as freely as I have with you and with Josh. I promise to think about what you said."

Mrs. Kirk smiled at her and held out her arm. "Come with me, dear," she invited. "We'll make the tea together."

The next morning Josh was already up when the two women entered the kitchen. Through the windows, Sherri could see the wash of sunshine transforming the flowerbeds into paintings of dazzling beauty.

"Hi, you two sleepyheads," Josh grinned, turning from the stove where he was spooning batter into the large iron skillet.

"Coffee's ready; pancakes will be in a few minutes," he said.

"Well, you'll certainly make some lucky woman a fine husband," Sherri bantered.

"You bet!" Josh said. "Jack of all trades and master of none."

When the three of them were seated around the table in the pleasant room, they found the pancakes to be light and mellow with just the right browned edges.

Passing the syrup, Sherri said, "All kidding aside, Josh, these are perfect."

"Well, eat up then," he answered, moving a melting pat of butter over the stack of cakes on his plate with a fork. "You and I are going to take a hike today."

Turning to Mrs. Kirk, he said, "Martha, would you be able to fix a couple of your delectable sandwiches for our picnic lunch?"

"Oh, Josh," she smiled, "you know I'll enjoy doing just that."

When Sherri went to get her sweater, Josh said quietly, "You might want to take a book along; you may have some waiting to do."

So instead of the sweater she had intended to wear, she took a long black cardigan with deep pockets. Into one she slipped a little book she had found on her bedside table and into the other, the notebook she kept in her uniform pocket when she was working.

As they were leaving, Josh called, "Don't expect us back until late afternoon, Martha."

The bright early morning sunshine was in their eyes until the street made a curve near the edge of town. Traffic was light, but they passed a school bus starting out to begin pick-ups as Josh headed the car into the countryside.

When they reached the Fairbanks' residence, Josh parked around the side of the house. "No need to arouse suspicion," he explained as they got out of the car.

When he began taking items from the backseat, Sherri asked, "Can I carry something for you?" She went around to his side of the car.

Josh nodded, handing her the picnic basket and a bright yellow hardhat.

"What's this, a miner's hat?"

"Very similar. It's also what cavers use. Comes in handy, although they rarely prevent injury if an overhead rock falls on you from any distance."

As they started to walk around the mansion, he went on, "In a low tunnel like the one I'm going to check this morning, a hardhat is great for not getting my head banged. It's also a help in short falls, usually."

"What about long falls?"

"You always hope you'll never make one of those, Sherri," he said very seriously. "When you fell into that chute, you were extremely fortunate that it had a gradually sloping area. That way, after a fall of two or three feet, you just slipped and skidded, sort of like a steep slide ride."

He smiled gently at her. "I know it wasn't as smooth a ride as on a slide, and I'm very thankful that you weren't seriously injured."

"Yes, me too. I was lucky that you were in the house and looked for me, then knew what to do when you found me."

When they reached the tree, Josh slipped the large coil of clothesline rope off his shoulder to the ground and un-rolled the bundle of clothes he'd been carrying.

Taking off his jacket, he slipped into a worn, heavy wool shirt. Then over his slim jeans he pulled on a pair of dungarees with thick rubber patches on the knees. His shirt sported similar patches. "I'll need some protection going through the low tunnel."

"You could pass for an automobile," Sherri giggled, touching an elbow patch.

"Almost," Josh chuckled. "After I finished Simpson's car last night, I cut up a piece of old tire-retread and glued the pieces on. They're awkward but they will do."

Taking a lap robe from the top of the picnic basket, he spread it on the ground next to the tree, then sat on a rock next to it.

"For you, madam, while I'm gone."

Removing a piece of yellow chalk and a pocketknife

from his pants pocket, Josh put them into his breastpocket and buttoned it. "Going into an unknown cave without another knowledgeable caver is risky at best. Since this is an emergency of sorts, I'm going in a short way to see if I can determine whether the cave may lead to what we're looking for. And you know where I'll be, so I wouldn't just disappear, in any event."

"What could I possibly do if something happened to you in there?" Sherri asked, worried.

"I'm pretty sure nothing will, because I'll keep going only when I know what's ahead, so don't worry." As he handed her a card he went on. "That card has a number for the National Cave Association. If I'm not back by midafternoon, please call them. But I promise you, Sherri, I'll be extra careful."

He checked the light with its small reflector clipped to the front part of the hardhat, then put the hat on his head and adjusted the chinstrap.

Anchoring the thin wire running from his helmet to the shoulder of his shirt with a safety pin, he slipped the battery pack into his empty breastpocket and carefully buttoned it.

Josh stood and checked his back pockets for the plastic bag of extra batteries and the small flashlight he'd put in them earlier.

"About ready," he said, patting the canteen on the back of his belt and bending to the swirl of rope.

He separated a heavier coil of rope from the other and slipped it over his shoulder, fastening it with a large clip. With the other coil in one hand, his floodlight-flash in the other, he headed for the cave. "Come on, Sherri, I want to explain something."

Sherri followed him to the opening where he was removing the large branch and armful of brush he had replaced the day before when they left.

"Just so you won't worry, I'm fastening one end of this

longer rope to the sapling just outside the entrance," he said, stooping to one knee to accomplish it even as he spoke.

"The loop on the other end I'll fasten around my ankle. As I maneuver inside, the rope will uncoil so you can tell how far I've gone. When it straightens, you'll know I'm in about two hundred feet. I may not be able to go even that far, so I could be back before you know I've left." He grinned at her reassuringly. "But to be honest, I hope that doesn't happen."

Sherri looked at him gratefully. "This rope sure relieves my mind. Will you start back when you reach two hundred feet?"

"Not unless I have to. If all is going well, and it seems absolutely safe ahead, I'll go on. I may signal you that I'm okay by calling, and I'll give the rope a couple of quick tugs."

"All right," Sherri answered, glad for Josh's thought-fulness. He was right when he thought she'd worry.

"If I'm not back in a decent time for lunch, start without me. I've plenty of water and a candy bar."

Noticing the concern still lingering on her face, he stepped toward her. With his hands on her shoulders, he looked intently into her eyes. "Thank you for your concern, Sherri. It feels good to matter to someone."

He gave her a quick smile, then dropping down onto his stomach, he crawled into the hole. In half a minute he had disappeared.

"Keep him safe, Lord," Sherri breathed as she crouched to look into the opening.

She saw a sudden surge of light as Josh switched his headlamp on. She stayed crouched until her legs began ach-ing, then sat down next to the little sapling with her back against the outcrop of rock to watch the rope as it slowly uncoiled.

Sherri lifted her gaze to the old walnut tree and beyond

it to where a hawk soared easily. A pair of squirrels bounded through the dried grasses and scampered up the tree, chattering wildly.

Suddenly the rope uncoiled very quickly for about seven or eight loops, then lay quietly.

Scrambling to her knees, she crawled the few feet to the opening and peered in, but she could see nothing at all, not even a faint glow from Josh's light.

Had he fallen? She was about to call when the rope began moving again, slowly but steadily now.

Relieved, she sat down again and pulled from her pocket the little book she'd borrowed from Mrs. Kirk.

She read for a while, the quietness broken only by an occasional bird or squirrel.

Feeling the sun beginning to shine on her face, she moved into the shade at the edge of the cave opening facing the sapling, so she could continue reading and keep an eye on the rope.

What sounded like a distant call from the cave made her snap to attention.

Looking up from the book, she saw the sapling jerk slightly. The rope was taut. As she watched, it slackened almost imperceptibly and tightened again.

Josh was signaling!

She heard a muffled, echoing call that sounded like "Okay."

She scrambled over and leaned into the opening. "Okay," she shouted back through cupped hands. His signal was meant to reassure her all was well. Nothing to do now but wait.

Sherri retrieved the book from where she'd dropped it, and went over to the tree where Josh had spread the blanket for her.

Lifting a corner of the cloth covering the picnic basket, she removed a glossy yellow apple. She took a bite of it and leaned back against the large trunk.

She finished the apple, and was trying to decide whether or not to have a sandwich when she noticed someone striding toward her across the field. Not Dodson again! Did this man spend his days stalking around the property following her? Josh wouldn't know he was here. What if he emerged from the cave while Dodson was still here? She'd have to get rid of him fast!

But as the man got closer, she saw that it was Arnie Morrow, fishing pole in hand. "Glad I found you, Miss McElroy," he said when he had reached her and dropped to the ground nearby. "Sherri, isn't it?"

Sherri nodded, smiling.

"I've been looking for you," he said. "I knew you were around because your car's parked at the Fairbanks' house, and you weren't in the house."

As she started to nod an assent, she cringed a bit inside as she heard the crackling of the bushes between them and the cave. Josh was coming out!

11

Arnie turned, his gaze following hers. "Who's over there?" he asked.

Sherri scrambled to her feet, wondering what to say.

Josh stood up, and Sherri breathed a sigh of relief. Apparently he had heard their voices and slipped off his caving garb before he stood. He stepped through the bushes and walked toward them, smiling.

"Oh, it's you, Stevens," Arnie said, extending his hand. "You surprised me."

Gripping Arnie's hand in a firm shake, Josh explained, "I just checked out what I thought might be an animal's den back there."

"Too bad it wasn't a cave," Arnie responded.

Josh looked at Sherri quickly, then back at Arnie. *How much did he know?*

"What do you know about caving?" Josh probed, trying to sound casual.

"Not a lot, not as much as I want to," Arnie answered, as the two sat on the ground near Sherri. "I've been in half a dozen times in Idaho when we lived there, and it intrigues me a lot. I tagged along on a mapping trip with friends in Washington, too, but it's not the kind of sport you can pursue just anywhere."

Sherri lifted the cloth from the picnic basket and spread it on the blanket. "Will you join us for lunch, Arnie?"

"I wouldn't want to barge in. I'm sure you only planned for two."

Josh broke in, chuckling, "Mrs. Kirk probably packed enough for half a dozen."

"Well, okay," Arnie said smiling, "I would like to stay."

"Look here," Sherri exclaimed. "She even wrapped a damp towel in plastic. Why don't you use it to clean up your face and hands, Josh?" she said, handing it to him.

"You look like a little boy who's been tumbling in a dirt pile," she added, giggling.

"Thanks," Josh said, taking it from her. "I *feel* that way, too."

Wiping his face, he asked Arnie, "Ever been caving around here anywhere?"

"No, as far as I know there aren't any closer than a hundred miles, although the terrain had me suspecting there might be."

"How long have you lived here?"

"Two and a half years. Been away at college most of that time, but I help the folks around the place here during vacations."

Josh nodded toward the pole balanced on a rock. "Looks like you were going fishing."

Arnie looked a bit sheepish. "Not exactly. I use that pole as a prop every once in a while."

"A prop?"

"Yes, which reminds me of why I was hunting for you, Sherri," Arnie answered, turning to her.

"Why were you?"

"I received a phone call from my mom, and—"

"Your mom?" Sherri interrupted. "Is she all right?"

"Sure, she's okay, I guess. Why do you ask?"

Seeing Josh's warning look, she said, "What connection do I have with her phone call?"

"Funny thing," Arnie answered. "Strange, really, not at all like her."

"What do you mean?" Josh asked.

"Well, she's such a calm, easygoing person usually, and she sounded excited, but mainly very tense."

"How do you mean?"

"She said she'd arrived at Aunt Gertrude's and wasn't sure how long she'd be away. My aunt had a stroke and wasn't doing well, so Mom went to be with her."

"When did she leave?" Sherri asked.

"Evidently the day before you came. Dad said he'd helped put her suitcase and things in the car before he left for Nobville. She wasn't here when I got home, and I didn't see Dad until the next day. Guess I was asleep when he got in that night."

Sherri was staring at him wide-eyed, then at Josh.

"How about some of those sandwiches, Sherri," Josh said. "Here, let me help serve this stuff. It looks great, and I'm hungry."

He poured hot chocolate from a big thermos into two thick white mugs, setting them on a large platter so they wouldn't tip. "I'll drink out of the thermos cup."

Sherri passed sandwiches on paper plates and opened the containers of salad and pickles, laying out cookies and pieces of fresh fruit.

After Josh prayed for their meal, they started eating, and Arnie said, "The strangest thing about my mom's call was the message for you, Sherri."

"Me?" Sherri asked, a forkful of salad halfway to her mouth, "but I don't know your mother."

"Well, I think it was for you. She asked if a young woman had arrived at the Fairbanks' house. When I told her about you, she told me to get a message to you that you might be in danger and should leave."

"That's all?" Josh asked.

"Yes, except that she said not to tell anyone else, and that she'd explain when she got back."

"Did you tell your dad?" Josh asked.

"No, I didn't. We've never been very close, though he's always treated me decently. Mom married him when I was still a kid, and since he'd never had any children, he gave me his name."

Arnie took a bite of his sandwich; then after a moment of silence, explained, "That was the reason for the fishing pole, to cover what I was really doing."

"Which was looking for Sherri?" Josh asked.

"Yes. People rarely ask you what your destination is when you're carrying a rifle or a fishing pole. They think it's obvious."

"Good idea," Josh said. "What do you think the danger is?"

"Haven't the slightest idea," Arnie answered. "But I've noticed that lawyer, Dodson, around here a number of times since Mr. Fairbanks has been away."

"Is it unusual for him to come?"

"Mom said it was when I asked her about it. Said she'd never seen him here before when Fairbanks wasn't here."

Arnie chewed a bite of sandwich, "Maybe Dodson could shed some light on what Mom may have meant. But I wouldn't want to ask him. I haven't cared much for him the times we've been face-to-face. He seems sort of devious. I don't mean to criticize the man, but I'm very uncomfortable around him for some reason."

Sherri glanced knowingly at Josh as she passed extra pickles. "Did you know Mr. Fairbanks very well, Arnie?" she asked.

"We were friends, I would say; although I haven't known him long, of course. He's a fine old fellow. We went fishing several times and had some good talks. He said I reminded him a bit of his son who left years ago."

Arnie took another bite of his sandwich and chewed thoughtfully, then said quietly, "He used to talk to me about my relationship to God. The first time anyone had done that. Actually, I had never thought about it. In that respect, Mr. Fairbanks is the best friend I have ever had, because he led me to a new life in the Lord. I also have him to thank for Emily."

"Emily?" Sherri questioned him.

"Emily Simmons, the girl I'm engaged to. Mr. Fairbanks knew her family and introduced us. She's working as a home economist in Indianapolis while I finish my degree at I.U. next year. She's really special."

"And pretty, too." Josh winked at him. "I saw you with her once at the station. What are your plans after graduating, besides marrying Emily, that is?"

"At this point, we're settling on working with troubled kids. My degree is in social work, and with Emily's background in nutrition and education, we see some good possibilities. And we're asking God to direct us."

"Do you think He will?" Sherri asked, honest surprise on her face.

"Emily thinks so, and I'm beginning to feel more sure about it, too, as I've continued to pray."

Josh looked at him with respect. "It must be great to be so sure about your future. I'd sure like to have as clear a plan as you have."

Sherri studied his face, as if seeing him in a new light. Was this the decision he had told Mrs. Kirk he was struggling with? Sherri had been so involved in her own problems, she hadn't given thought to his concerns.

"What would you like to do with your life, Josh?" she asked him.

Taking an oatmeal cookie from the package in front of him, Josh was slow to answer.

"Like I said, I'm not sure. But what you said, Arnie, about working with troubled kids sure clicks with me, too. I spent last summer on an inner-city volunteer project, and I've never seen people in such need. I grew up without a dad, but at least I had a loving, Christian mom, and a clean, happy place to live. Most of these kids have nothing, not even basic medical care."

"You may have missed your calling," Sherri said with a smile. "Sounds to me like you'd make a fine, compassionate physician."

Josh looked at her. "Interesting you'd say that, Sherri. I've thought recently of medical school, but I'm just not sure if it's what God wants me to do.

"But thanks for being concerned," he said, and for a moment they looked into each other's eyes, oblivious to Arnie's presence.

Arnie cleared his throat. "I . . . uh . . . I think I'll leave you two alone. I have things to do." Sherri and Josh dropped their gaze, embarrassed, as Arnie rose and started for his fishing pole.

"Wait a minute, Arnie," Josh said, glancing at Sherri while he drained his cup, "I want to show you something. I feel like we can trust you."

Sherri gathered up the picnic things and followed them.

Arnie was on his stomach a short way inside the tunnel.

"And this is where you were earlier?" he asked, backing out, Josh's clothes and hardhat in tow.

"Yes," Josh answered. "There's evidently quite a labyrinth in there. This section leads downward at a fairly gentle slope after it makes a sharp corner about eight feet in. Then after a slightly larger crawlway, there's a short drop of about ten feet—"

"That's when the rope suddenly uncoiled so fast?" Sherri interrupted.

"Probably, but I was controlling it. There was no danger. After that, you can walk upright. But there are a number of corridors angling off. It's a fascinating place."

Turning to Sherri, he said, "I found what I was looking

for; just a second." Josh bent under one of the large bushes growing in front of the cave area and pulled out the leather packet.

"Josh! You mean you went back down that—?"

"No, Sherri," he broke in. "I had no trouble finding it. You must have dropped it before you thought you did."

"Yes," she said, remembering falling on her knees just after the candle was extinguished.

Arnie looked very confused, "You mean you've both been in there before?" he asked.

"Just for a short time," Josh answered. "When do you have to be back at college?"

"I have the rest of this week off."

"I'd appreciate your not telling anyone about this cave right now, Arnie. Think you'd like to check it out with me?"

"Would I!" Arnie grinned. "Most definitely."

"Can you get away tomorrow?"

"Tomorrow's fine."

"Good, bring any equipment you have and meet us here tomorrow morning about five."

"Great! See you later, Sherri, and thanks for lunch," he said, picking up his pole.

Josh wrapped his cave shirt and jeans carefully around his mining hat, being sure to conceal the rubber patches.

"No use arousing anyone's suspicion. We're fortunate Arnie seems to be an all-right guy. Even sounds like he's a Christian. And my grandfather liked him. That's why I decided to tell him about the cave. Besides, we need his help."

"Yes, I understood," Sherri said.

Opening the pouch, she asked, "What about the letter and watch. Would you like to see them now?"

"Let's wait until we're back at Martha's. But Sherri, let's not say anything to her or to Arnie about the treasure. At least not yet." She nodded in agreement.

They had barely finished folding the lap robe to start back to the car when Ross Morrow came from around the edge of the hill, binoculars swinging from a strap around his neck.

12

*M*orrow's face seemed to express suspicion thinly disguised by a forced friendliness.

"What ya doin' way over here?"

"We were having a picnic," Josh said, raising the basket in explanation.

"Uh," Morrow grunted. "Why here?"

"We went on a hike before we ate," Josh said. "Are you a bird watcher?"

"A what?"

"I noticed the binoculars, and wondered if you were bird watching."

Morrow was obviously flustered by the question, but answered nothing. Forcing a smile of sorts, he turned to Sherri, "What was so interesting over by the hill earlier today? Saw you sitting there for a while." He waved in that direction.

"Oh, I was reading a book while I waited for Josh to join me for lunch," Sherri answered. "When the sun began to get in my eyes, I moved over under that tree."

"Where was you?" Morrow directed the question sharply at Josh.

"I was busy this morning, but I finished what I had to do in time to join Sherri," Josh answered easily. Sherri admired his quick explanation. It was completely truthful, yet revealed nothing they didn't want known.

Ross Morrow's countenance was slowly losing its look of distrust.

Sherri reached for the basket, taking it from Josh. "Mr. Morrow, we have a sandwich and some cookies left. Would you care to share them?"

"Naw, naw . . . I got things to do," he waved her off.

"Well, goodbye then," she said, handing the basket back to Josh.

As she and Josh were walking away, she turned to see Morrow shuffling off toward the pine grove.

"I wonder how long he'd been watching us," Sherri said.

"My thought exactly. I'm curious as to whether he saw Arnie here, and the activity at the cave opening."

"He didn't even glance in that direction after asking what I had been doing there," Sherri said.

"Yes, I was aware of that, too. Maybe I'm just getting jumpy, but I'm going to camouflage it again after he's gone. We can wait behind the forsythia bushes until he's out of sight."

Their wait was short, and retracing their steps, Josh put down the basket and clothes bundle and went over to the opening.

Sherri followed him. "What do you think he'll do if he did see both of us here? Why do you think he was interested?"

"I have no idea," Josh answered, "but since this cave has some special connection to my grandfather's house, I'd much rather keep it a secret, especially from him."

When they arrived back in town, Josh stopped first at the station.

"I'll take over here," he said, "and you can drive Martha back to the house."

Inside the station, Mrs. Kirk sat knitting in a small rocker between a rack of fan belts and a stack of tires. She looked up with a smile.

"How did your day go? You both look as though the

fresh air did you a world of good. And you certainly don't look as peaked as you did, dear," she said, looking at Sherri.

"It was great, Martha," Josh said, "and the lunch was especially nice. I'll take over here now and you can go home."

"No," Martha said, continuing to knit, "I started a pot roast before I came back at noon, so if you two will put in the potatoes and carrots—they're all peeled and in a bowl of water—and prepare a salad, I'll be over about six o'clock. Simpson's teenage son is stopping by in a while to discuss the possibility of working here some this summer."

Mrs. Kirk gave them another warm smile and waved them out.

After Sherri had taken care of the vegetables and Josh had set the table, they went into the living room and sat on the couch. Then they opened the leather packet Josh had retrieved from the cave.

Turning the watch over in his hands he said, "This does match the carving on that bedroom door. I suppose it began as my great-great-grandmother's room years ago, since Grandfather told you the watch originally belonged to *his* grandfather."

Opening the watchcase, he added, "You were correct about the Scripture inscription being from Job, Sherri—and it is the same one as on the frame, the one about the treasure of the snow."

Josh sat lost in thought for a minute, then, "You know, Sherri, whatever the connection is between this verse and the cave, someone tried very definitely to convey the meaning. But what connection do snow and treasure have?"

"Maybe the letter will explain what it all means."

"Right." He emptied the other contents of the pouch between them on the sofa.

Josh picked up the fragile letter, browning with age. It made a soft crackling sound when he handled it, and bits of the edges broke off as he started to unfold it.

Although he proceeded carefully, the brittle paper split at the creases. Josh nudged them gently with his fingers, trying to align them correctly, but pieces kept breaking off.

"Wait, Josh," Sherri said, pulling her notebook from her sweater pocket. "If we had some glue, we could stabilize the pieces with a backing and then reassemble the sheets."

"Good thinking, Sherri. I have some tape that should do the job."

As he returned from his room, tape in hand, Sherri said, "I've carefully slipped a sheet from my notebook under each piece, so we don't have to handle them and risk damaging them more."

"That was a good idea," Josh answered. "The writing is so faded, we may have trouble deciphering it as it is, without having a jigsaw puzzle to put together, too."

When he had finished gently taping the edges of the pieces to the heavier sheets, Josh said, "How about slipping these into your book to flatten them a bit? It'll make reading them easier."

Sherri carefully placed the sheets between the pages of her notebook and laid a heavy book on top to add weight, while Josh fingered the beautiful gold watch, impressed by its fine detail.

As Sherri bent to pet the elderly gray cat that had ambled in from the kitchen, she exclaimed, "Josh, here's another folded paper! Do you suppose it's yours, that it fell to the floor without our noticing it?"

"It's possible," he said, taking it from her. "But it certainly isn't as old as the other one. It may be something of Martha's."

"I don't think so; we'd have noticed it when we sat down. I think you should open it. Then let's read the old one next. It will take too long for the pieces to really flatten."

Josh nodded and unfolded the sheet of crisp, white paper.

"The date is just two months ago," he said. Then he read aloud:

For Joshua, my grandson.

Enclosed is a letter from my own grandfather to me. The summer after my fifteenth birthday we used the gold key to take a marvelous, exciting trip to a spot I had not known existed. I didn't take that trip again until I was in my late twenties. At that time, I took the same route with a young lady and her brother. That lady later became my wife. I loved her dearly; I've missed her sorely.

We made two maps and in later years tried to make the travel route more accessible. I'm enclosing one map with this; the other is in a different form and on the trip route itself. You will find it there, I'm sure, in case this one is lost or stolen.

I am telling you these things so you can discover your inheritance in the event we do not meet on earth, and I am unable to discuss it with you in person. I've had a strong feeling lately that I may not, after all my efforts and dreams, have opportunity to tell you these things face-to-face; and that most of all, though we have not met, you are greatly loved.

I've tried to manage well the businesses my grandfather left for me. I am leaving them to missionary groups and charities. The other legacy he left, I leave for you on the trip-route, saying as he did, "With all you have, honor God."

Joshua Stevens Fairbanks

"Sounds as though I had a fine, considerate grandfather, doesn't it?" Josh said quietly.

Sherri nodded. Taking the loose sheets with the attached fragments, she laid them carefully between them on the couch.

"Let's piece these together. Although it's faint, the writing is still legible."

After rearranging the papers several times until the words made sense, Josh again read aloud:

April 8, 1910
Joshua, my grandson,

You were born early this morning on my sixtieth birthday.

When I was a very young man, I accumulated a fortune in California. I will be an old man by the time you reach maturity, so I'm planning that when you're about fifteen years old, I'll show you the key and explain how I've arranged for the fortune's use. I trust I will live until then; may God grant this prayer.

Josh stopped reading and said to Sherri, with a soft smile on his face, "It's a strange feeling, reading a letter that my great-great-grandfather wrote to my own grandfather, someone with my own name. It's almost as though he were writing down through the years directly to me."

Glancing back at the assembled sheets, he continued reading:

I have never told your father the secret. I have given him more than enough for his lifetime; my son is not as wise in spending as I would like. It is you, little one, on whom I pin my hopes, my dreams, and my prayers for the far future.

Use the hidden treasure to assist the needy and the homeless, as I have been able to do without anyone but God knowing. I want no thanks from the world.

However, use it in whatever ways He directs you; His plans are greater than mine.

The important thing to remember is to surrender to Him your life, all your assets. Listen to His directions in your heart, trusting Him completely. In all you do, try to glorify Him.

Your loving grandfather,
Martin Steven Fairbanks.

"Strange, isn't it," Sherri said, "your great-great-grandfather wanting to help the poor and homeless, and now you having the same desire."

Josh nodded and Sherri could see tears in his eyes when he looked up. "What seems coincidence in our lives is often God's advance planning, I think," he said.

With a smile he added, "I wish I could have known these two men. They have left me a spiritual legacy that can't be compared with the monetary one. I'm glad they had their priorities right."

Josh gingerly picked up the sheet he had just put down, "Sherri, there's a P.S. here. It's so faint that I almost missed it."

Holding the sheet closer to his eyes, then switching on the floor lamp at his end of the couch, he read:

You may one day be interested, little Grandson, in how the Fairbanks property came to be ours. I was stalking a wild turkey on a fine Saturday afternoon in the year 1866, when I came upon a small entrance which led me to the great unexplored area. Because of my wealth, I was able to purchase the large tract of land and build my home over that entrance which I later enlarged and incorporated into part of the building's construction. A particularly beautiful spot in the unseen area became the place where I placed a portion of your inheritance.

Josh stopped reading and, while he was carefully stacking the sheets of paper in order, Sherri went to the kitchen to check the progress of the dinner.

When Josh joined her, he said, "There are two things nagging at my mind. One is about the dead woman you saw. If it wasn't Mrs. Morrow, who was it? Also, how did the body disappear? And to where?"

"I wondered about that, too," Sherri said, "when Arnie told us about his mother's phone call. But it had bothered me before that—the disappearance, I mean."

Sherri walked from the stove to where Josh sat on a tall stool near the window. "There's something else, Josh, concerning your grandfather's things. The one letter said there were maps. It said one would be on the trip; that would mean in the cave, I suppose. But he said he was enclosing the other map, yet it wasn't there."

"That's right. I was so surprised by what was in the letter I didn't think about that," Josh said.

He took the packet from his jacket pocket and put it on the table. He untied the thong and took out the things they had examined earlier. He slid his hand inside the old leather pouch, feeling carefully.

"There's nothing else there, Sherri. Take a look."

She checked with her hand as he had done and peered carefully inside to see if there might be a concealed compartment.

Replacing the letter, watch, and key, she asked, "What do you think happened to it?"

"Happened to what?" Martha asked, coming in the door.

13

"Just a paper, Martha," Josh said, moving quickly to obstruct her view of the leather pouch on the table. "Supper is almost ready. I'll pour the milk while Sherri dishes things up if you want to relax in the living room for a few minutes."

"How nice," Mrs. Kirk said, smiling cheerily. "Jerry Simmons came a little early, so I decided to close up and come on home when he left. My customers know where to find me if they want something."

The older woman turned and headed toward her bedroom as Sherri and Josh exchanged looks of relief. Josh picked up the pouch. "Think I'll stash this in my room for now," he told Sherri. By the time he returned, Sherri had dinner on the table.

Later as they were finishing the dessert, Mrs. Kirk asked, "What do you two have planned for tomorrow? There's nothing waiting in the garage, and I can stay at the station again, so I thought Josh might like to show you around our area, Sherri. There are some flower displays at the conservatory in Pikesville."

"Actually, Martha, there is something interesting I'd like her to see, some natural rock formations in the hills. We've already invited Arnie Morrow to go with us. I appreciate your suggestion, though. We'll leave by five, if that's okay with Sherri."

Sherri's eyes sparkled as she whispered, "I can go along?"

Josh nodded. "You could use some old clothes since we might be getting very dirty. Do you have anything grubby with you?"

"You know, Josh," Mrs. Kirk broke in, "there's a pair of Peter Junior's almost-new coveralls in the bottom drawer of the dresser in your room. He was much smaller than you. I'm sure they'd come near to fitting Sherri. If you'll get them and put them on the bed in my room, she can try them on."

"Thanks, Martha," he smiled.

When he returned to the kitchen, Mrs. Kirk said to Sherri, "Go try them on and let's see what altering they need."

Sherri hurried to the bedroom, quickly put on the coveralls, and came back to stand before them. "How's this?" she asked with a giggle.

"Oh, Sherri," Mrs. Kirk said, joining her laughter, "I guess you're not as tall as I thought you were."

Sherri looked down at the rolled up sleeves and pant cuffs and the too-ample torso area. "They're not too bad. I'll wear a belt and pin the cuffs up."

Turning around in full circle, she asked, "Seriously, they'll work okay. Don't you think so, Josh?"

"Sure will. Just take up the looseness a little, so you don't get caught on some rock."

"I'll help you with it," Mrs. Kirk said, getting up to answer the phone.

"It's Arnie, Josh. He says he has an extra helmet Sherri can use if she hasn't one. And I told him that if he doesn't mind the drive in to town, I want him to come for breakfast in the morning before you start out."

"Hi, Arnie," Josh said, after taking the phone. "The helmet will be great. Now we have her all outfitted. Wait'll you see her tomorrow." He chuckled, looking teasingly at Sherri as he hung up.

The next morning, Josh was waiting outside the house when Arnie drove up. Opening the car door as Arnie cut the motor, Josh told him, "Mrs. Kirk's been bustling around the kitchen for half an hour. Sure smells good in there."

Entering the kitchen, Arnie said to his hostess, "It sure was nice of you to invite me." Then grinning at Josh and Sherri, he added, "I don't imagine these two minded a bit that you insisted on getting up before dawn to fix breakfast for us before we leave."

Sherri wrinkled her nose at him as she placed a plate of warm biscuits on the table next to a platter of bacon and eggs.

"I had packed a few items for today's lunch before I talked to you," Arnie said to Mrs. Kirk. "But I had expected to go without breakfast. This is great."

"Well, you all need a good meal if you're going to spend the day walking and climbing," she answered. "And I want you to come back for supper with us, too, Arnie."

"In that case, Arnie," Josh said, "we can ride out together."

Later, when they entered the Fairbanks' driveway, Arnie said, "Take this little cutoff here. Instead of going up to the front of the house, this will take us back behind the old stable, nearer to where we're going."

They hiked across the field from the stable in the early daylight, the two young men carrying the helmets and heavy coils of rope. Sherri toted the picnic basket Mrs. Kirk had insisted on sending.

"I didn't want to tell her this would be bulky and inconvenient because we were going to crawl into a cave," she said. "I was afraid she would worry."

Arnie motioned his head toward the extra helmet under his free arm. "I brought along some small empty nylon packs; they're stuffed here in Sherri's helmet. Wasn't sure if you had any. We can put the sandwiches in them and fasten them to the back of our belts. There's an extra filled canteen, too, and some batteries."

When they approached the cave, Josh told Arnie about Ross finding them there the previous day.

"That's strange," Arnie said. "I didn't know Dad had binoculars, and I can't imagine why he'd be upset at your being here."

They became involved then in arranging the gear comfortably and explaining to Sherri how to best avoid scrapes and bumps during the crawl through the entrance tunnel.

As the three put on work gloves, Sherri said, "It was nice of Mrs. Kirk to loan me her gloves and heavy boots. And I appreciate your putting patches on these knees for me, Josh. After the scraping my legs got the other day, I'll need them."

Josh entered the cave first and Sherri followed. She dropped to her stomach and pulled herself forward on her elbows.

"Remember to keep your head down, Sherri," Josh said. "We can raise to our knees after about twenty feet. This low portion doesn't extend very far."

But it seemed terribly long to Sherri. Her shoulders ached and her elbows were sore by the time they reached the part high enough to crawl in. Then it was one hand and knee forward, the other hand and knee forward, over and over with deliberateness.

She heard her helmet scrape the ceiling every so often, even though she tried to keep her head scrunched between her shoulders. And the walls felt very close, seeming to narrow more and more as they progressed. Sherri felt claustrophobic and wondered if she was going to panic.

Just as she was about to tell Josh that she wanted to go back, he stopped crawling and shouted, "There's a small pile of rubble here; then you'll make a turn to the left. Soon we can stand."

Grateful that he had spoken at that moment, Sherri resolved to keep going. She would push away thoughts of the hundreds of tons of soil in the hill above her head. She felt very tense, yet at the same time irritated at herself for her apprehension.

Then, pushing her feelings of embarrassment aside, she called, "Josh, could we please stop for a minute. I need a short rest."

"Sure, we could all use it. Just stay where you are and put your head on your arms for a bit." Then speaking louder, "Did you hear that, Arnie?"

"Sure did," Arnie called back.

In a few minutes, they started crawling again. When Sherri reached the rubble of stones, she had to drop to her stomach again in order to squeeze between it and the ceiling. She was breathing heavily by the time she reached the other side, so she dropped her head to rest again briefly.

"Wow," she said loudly, so Josh could easily hear her, "weren't you scared when you came in yesterday, not knowing where this led or what might be in here?"

Josh chuckled. "Scared isn't exactly the right word, but it comes close. A lot of excitement and anticipation is mixed in, too, the first time you enter an unknown cave like this. But it's sort of fun, too, don't you agree?"

"I suppose so," Sherri answered, not really convinced.

She raised to her knees again and began the one-knee, one-hand-forward routine, trying to push from her mind the proximity of the walls that seemed to press in on her.

The close quarters kept reminding her, with each foot of progress, that she was going farther and farther into the earth. Only Josh ahead of her and Arnie behind kept her thinking sensibly.

"Okay, Sherri," Josh said as she almost bumped into

him, "you can rest again. There's room enough to sit up now without stooping."

Lifting her head slightly to see him, she saw that the ceiling was a bit higher here, and her helmet wasn't bumping it at all.

Josh was sitting with his legs dangling over the edge of a hole about nine feet across.

"When I came out yesterday," Josh said, sliding the rope onto his lap, "I noticed some foot and handholds cut into the rock wall below us here and used them on my return. If you're okay, I'm going down now. It's a short drop."

Wrapping the end of one of the ropes behind his back and under his arms, he looped it over an upright boulder next to him, and disappeared over the side.

Sherri scooted over to where he had been sitting and looked down.

She felt a cool draft against her face from where Josh stood just below her. In the circle of illumination cast by his helmet light, he was refastening the loose rope to the large coil he'd pulled down after him.

Raising his arms, he said, "Sherri, Arnie can help you lower yourself over the side. I'll put your foot into the step and lift you the rest of the way down."

Determined to not let them know she was afraid of slipping, Sherri did as she was told.

She slid easily from Arnie's grasp over the edge, felt Josh positioning her foot, then found herself sliding through his arms and standing on the smooth rock floor below.

By the time she had composed herself, Arnie was beside them.

The hole was widened slightly at the bottom from about four feet above the floor, so it was roomy enough to move around easily even with the large coils of rope on the floor about them. Quickly rearranging them over their shoulders, Josh looked at her. "Ready for another section?"

he asked. "There's a short time of stooping, but we'll be through it in about a minute."

Sherri nodded, smiling to cover her apprehensions. Bending over, she followed Josh through a tunnel of smooth walls that curved to a rounded ceiling just above their shoulders.

Her neck was beginning to ache when Josh stated, "It's okay to stand up now," and Sherri raised her head to gaze at a completely unexpected sight.

They stood just inside a large room of rock, its floor and ceiling crowded with strange rocky shapes and bulges.

"There's an opening on the far side," Josh said. "Watch your step, now, until we get through this chamber. There's a clearer area on this side," he added, waving at them to follow.

As they approached the opposite side of the cavern, all Sherri could see was a narrow slit about seven feet high.

"We're not going through that, are we?" she gulped.

"Yes, we are," Josh responded. "It's a squeezeway, but there's more than enough room to slip through sideways.

"Actually, even a fairly husky person could get through if he really wanted to." Sensing Sherri's discomfort, he added, "It's a narrow passage that extends only about ten or twelve feet."

He started to enter, then turning to her, asked, "Do close places bother you?"

"Well, they're not my first choice," Sherri answered with a feeble laugh.

"I'll reach back and hold your hand," Josh encouraged, "and Arnie can take your other one. We'll slip through together. You two can switch off your lights until we get through. It curves a bit to the left, so we'll move slowly. It's close in spots."

Sherri gripped Josh's hand and stepped into the opening. Arnie clasped her other hand and they inched slowly along. The rough rock wall stood just inches from her face as it forced her breath back at her; she could feel the opposite wall hard against her back. The strong hands she felt through her gloves were reassuring in the close darkness of the narrow place.

When she turned her head to face in the direction they were edging, she could see the silhouette of Josh's head and shoulders against the glow of his light, which he had dimmed.

Quite suddenly, it seemed, they were in another large space, an oval, high-ceilinged expanse formed eons ago from the underground rock.

Sherri switched her helmet light back on. The walls looked like swirling water forever solidified in stone, and far above her, she saw what appeared to be thin, convoluted draperies of some sort of pink-tinged mineral hanging in voluminous folds from the distant ceiling.

"I never dreamed a place like this existed," she remarked, awestruck.

"This is only the beginning," Josh returned as he started across the uneven floor of the cavern.

"Are these tall formations stalactites?" Sherri asked Arnie, who was beside her.

"No, they're called stalagmites. Those icicle-shaped growths on parts of the ceiling are stalactites. Actually, speleothem is the word used to describe the mineral deposits you're seeing."

He paused. "Geology 101," he grinned with a wink.

"That's interesting, Arnie. I recall reading about these in school, but I've never seen them before. And each one seems different from the others. Look at those tiny ones here, and those over there must be ten feet tall."

"Yes, and there are some especially long stalactites hanging from the ceiling just above some of them. Sometimes they eventually grow together and form columns."

"Come on, you two," Josh called, "we have a lot to see today." His voice echoed several times, then seemed to roll in again from somewhere in the unseen distance.

Walking carefully, following the beam of Arnie's flashlight, they admired the formations they passed, until they reached Josh near a jutted-out section of wall near the midportion of the huge place.

"Follow me," Josh commanded with a smile. "After we get in, there's a smooth, straight section that goes for quite a distance." They followed him around a stalagmite the size of a man and entered an archway.

As he had said, the corridor beyond was level underfoot and seemed almost like walking through a poorly lighted subway tunnel. The sound of their boots echoed with muffled resonance.

Sherri marveled at the beauty of the speleothems growing from the walls and ceiling as Josh spotlighted them with his floodlight-flash. Each one was uniquely shaped, some glowing in twisted forms, others looking like piles of sparkling gems.

Then, just as they went through another arch onto a broad ledge, Sherri heard it.

"It's the water, Josh!" she exclaimed, "exactly as I heard it the other day, only much louder."

"Yes, it's just below us somewhere. I scooted to the edge yesterday, but I couldn't see the bottom, and I didn't have a flare to drop to get a better view. It sounds as though it may be two hundred feet or so down, but sounds become distorted in a cave, so I may be wrong."

"Are you planning to go down there?" Sherri asked.

"No, not today at least," he answered, "but I wouldn't let you go along anyway, Sherri, so don't worry about it."

As Sherri followed Josh along the ledge, with Arnie right behind her, she kept close to the fluted wall rising vertically above her to a ceiling she could not see. Occasionally, water dripped from that unseen space above, making the footing slippery and uncertain.

There was a feeling of damp chill, and she shivered as she thought of what it might be like to suddenly slip and go over the edge of the precipice lying just to her right.

But Josh and Arnie seemed unconcerned, so she said nothing about her fear, although the ten-foot-wide ledge on which they walked seemed much narrower as she followed along the uneven surface.

Suddenly Josh stopped. "This ledge continues for several hundred feet yet, and there are at least two passages leading from it. This first one leads to the spot you originally started from the other day," he stated, pointing to the opening beside him and turning to Sherri, cautioning her with a look to say nothing about the bookcase opening into the cave.

"It climbs and eventually makes a right angle where another corridor leads to the spot where you fell."

Then, turning back to continue along the ledge, he added, "I don't think we should take time for that one today. I want you to see this other area."

Going on past the opening which led to dense darkness, Sherri shuddered, remembering her fall into the shaft.

Josh stopped again shortly and shined his light into another opening. "This is it. Careful now, it slopes downward, but not very steeply."

They entered, and before long Sherri realized that the rushing sound of the river had waned to a slight whisper.

Peering ahead, she saw that they were entering another place of wonder. As they ascended a slight rise, she found that around and before her the walls were scalloped in waves of pale gray interspersed with formations of startling white.

Turning a corner after following Josh in a detour around a massive pile of what he called "breakdown," Sherri found herself in another, even larger, passage.

Ahead and to her right, on a steep slope carved from dark brown rock, she saw stump-like stalagmites rising in varying heights. Her steps slowed almost to a standstill as she gazed at them in passing. Beyond them, she stood awed before an overhead ledge of rippling cream and white on which Josh was playing his light.

Soon they came to a tiny stream only about two feet wide, emerging from a slit low in the rock wall. It made barely a sound as it moved, continuing along the edge of the passage. It meandered quietly beside them, then suddenly dropped easily over a foot-high waterfall, flowing into a wide, still pool circled with a crust of shimmering white.

"God sure has made some incredible things. Too bad not many besides Him will ever get to see something like this," Josh said softly. "I think of that every time I explore caves, and it's sure helped me realize more fully how amazing His creative power really is."

Stooping to view the pool more closely, he continued, "I'm afraid that too often I get so caught up in my daily life that I forget His vast creation, and more importantly, the needs of people around me."

Neither Sherri nor Arnie answered, but he didn't seem to expect them to.

They skirted the splendid spot and found the stream forming again where it flowed slowly out of the pool over a low sculptured wall of white brilliant flowstone.

Sherri gasped, "Each thing is more exquisite than the last. Oh, I'm so glad I came! Thank you for bringing me along, Josh."

"I'm glad you're enjoying it, Sherri," Josh replied, turning to look directly into her sparkling eyes. Even in the strange mixture of light and shadow, she could see that special tenderness she had seen before in his gaze.

Then, his voice taking a lighter tone, he said, "She's a good sport, isn't she, Arnie?"

"Yes, she is," Arnie answered from where he was closely inspecting a speleothem that looked like a mass of glass needles.

"The next area is not as beautiful," Josh said, "but in its own way, it's awe-inspiring." Josh led them over a low area of breakdown to a small opening between two boulders.

"This is a duck-under, but you can stand straight immediately afterward," he said, bending over and going through the small space. Turning, he directed his flashlight on the floor so Sherri could see clearly where to step as she emerged on the other side.

The three of them stood quietly gazing around at the expanse before them, straining to see as far as the beams of their headlamps and flashlights could penetrate.

Then they began walking forward among columns like giant redwood trees from floor to ceiling. It was very quiet except for the movement of their feet and the soft sounds of their breathing.

"It seems like a silent, deserted, petrified forest," Sherri whispered.

"I didn't check yesterday for what may extend beyond this cavern," Josh said, "and we won't today, but I hope I have another opportunity sometime."

"Me, too," Arnie said. "This is awesome."

Before going back, they decided to rest and eat the sandwiches and cookies Mrs. Kirk had provided. Arnie added the fruit and peanuts he had brought.

Sherri studied the strong profile of Josh's handsome face as he gazed at the formations around them.

If there was a treasure hidden in this cave, they hadn't come much closer to uncovering it, Sherri thought. But for her, the friendship she'd found with this kind, caring man was as special as any treasure. Leaving Josh was not going to be easy.

A while later, when they were preparing to continue back after eating their lunch, Sherri asked, "Do you suppose Indians ever lived in these caves?"

"It's possible they may have used them for shelters or storage. They did in some areas of the country," Josh said.

"Well, look at this," Sherri said, pointing to a flat rock about the size of a man's hand lying next to where she had been sitting. "There are marks on it."

"They probably don't mean anything, Sherri."

"Maybe not," she said, "but I've seen several others just like them today. They didn't really register in my mind until I saw this one. They must have been markers for something. Always three dots or little circles. It's strange."

Josh and Arnie both inspected the flat rock, then replaced it exactly where it had been.

"Whatever it was for," Josh said, "I don't want to disturb it. A lot of valuable and interesting facts about our country's history or land are ruined by unthinking people. Often a cave's environment is disrupted or defaced by misuse, too. My chalk marks on our route are an example. When we've finished exploring, I'll wipe them off the walls. I usually use fluorescent tape, because it strips off easily when you're done exploring, but I didn't have any."

Arnie chuckled, "Some fellows told me that packrats have been known to remove those fluorescent markers before the caver makes a return trip."

"I've heard that, too," Josh said with a chuckle. "It could cause a real problem, but at least the tape doesn't damage anything."

On their return trip, they moved at a more leisurely pace, taking time to closely examine some of the formations that were easily accessible.

When they had reached the last crawl-space tunnel, and Sherri was again holding her head low while doing her one-knee, one-hand-forward crawl, she began to realize how tired she was.

She stopped to rest just after pulling herself over and around the pile of rubble before the shorter stretch to the entrance-exit opening. Josh was already out of sight, and Arnie had lagged behind, wanting to practice on the hand-foot-hold climb a time or two.

Sherri thought she heard voices, then remembered what Josh had said about cave-sound distortion, and dismissed the thought. But when she pulled herself out of the cave opening on her stomach a few minutes later, she saw an extra pair of men's boots standing not far from Josh's.

Quickly scrambling to her feet, she stared wide-eyed and unbelieving at the gun Ross Morrow pointed menacingly at Josh.

14

Morrow took a step toward Josh and waved the gun close to his face. "You're snoopin'. I seen it with my own eyes."

As Sherri turned to slip back into the safety of the cave, her helmet knocked against a branch and fell to the ground. Morrow turned slightly, "So, you're here too, are you, girlie? Well, you two can't fool me. You're huntin' something, I'll bet. Dodson told me somebody might try to steal something valuable of Fairbanks'."

"Dodson?" Josh asked. "Why would he think that? Have there been problems here? Has someone broken into the house?"

"He didn't say," Morrow growled. "And what business is it of yours anyway?"

"I've told you that Joshua Fairbanks is my grandfather. I have a right to be here as a family member," Josh stated firmly. "You need some proof of my identity? Will my driver's license satisfy you?"

"I dunno, from what I hear on TV, it's not so hard to get a forged license if a guy wants one bad enough. And sometimes when there's lots of cash involved, some guys do."

"Well, I didn't get mine that way," Josh said, irritation edging his voice.

Morrow seemed uncertain, shifting back and forth on his feet and lowering the gun slightly.

Josh removed his wallet from his pocket and flipped it open, holding it out toward Morrow.

Morrow scrutinized it a moment, then handed it back, grudgingly mollified, and pocketed his firearm. He moved closer to the low, oblong opening in the side of the hill. "Even if you are Fairbanks' relative, and I ain't sayin' yet that I believe you are, that still don't seem a good reason for all the queer places I find you in, and I think Dodson will want to hear about it."

"What has Dodson got to do with us?" Josh asked.

"Maybe nothin'. But he's the big cheese here as far as takin' care of Fairbanks' business."

Josh looked at him quizzically, but said nothing.

Ross Morrow walked back closer to one of the tall bushes secluding the cave opening and peered over, "What's this, a cave?"

"Seems to be," Josh answered.

"I've heard there used to be bears in this area," Morrow said. "Think there's any still around?" he asked, backing away.

"There's always a possibility," Josh answered, trying to look convincingly serious.

"That space sure looked big enough to house a bear, maybe several." Morrow took another step back, fear edging into his voice. "Dodson will want to investigate this himself. Me, I've got better things to do. But you better talk to Dodson about whether it's all right for you to be pokin' around all over the place." And as he headed quickly away, Josh and Sherri heard him mumble, "Wait'll Dodson hears about this. Looks suspicious to me."

Josh shook his head, then smiled at Sherri, his eyes warm with sincerity. "I'm thankful you weren't so hard to convince about who I am."

Sherri returned his warmth. Then, deeply aware of the

magnetic pull, she looked away, uncertain about her growing attraction toward him.

Although she felt far from light-hearted, she said teasingly, "Maybe I convince too easily."

A few moments later, Arnie pulled himself out of the cave, and Josh and Sherri told him about their conversation with his father. "I don't know what's gotten into him, or what he's got to do with Dodson. I wasn't aware that they were more than passing acquaintances. I'm sorry, Josh. You too, Sherri."

"It's not your fault, Arnie," Josh said, "but I wish I knew what this was all about."

After throwing a couple of branches across the opening, they headed across the field toward the stable where Josh's car was parked. They were tired and all three were silent, immersed in their own questions about the past few hours.

The sun had set and dusk was closing in as Josh drove past the landscaped expanse of lawn nearest the mansion and followed the little side road around the curve where they would enter the main drive.

"There's a light on in Mr. Fairbanks' house," Sherri said. "On the second floor. I wonder if Mrs. Morrow is back?"

Instead of taking the bend toward the highway, Josh turned and followed the long drive to the front of the mansion. A black Oldsmobile was parked in the drive.

"It's obviously not my mom," Arnie said.

Parking and getting out, Josh said, "Let's check it out."

After she had stepped from the car, Sherri turned to where Arnie sat in the backseat. "Coming?"

"No, I think I'll stay here and see who comes out in case you miss them."

"Right," Josh said. "We won't be long."

As they walked up to the house, he said, "I want to

check quickly, too, through those business papers in the desk. Maybe they'll reveal some information about my grandfather's affairs that will help make sense of all this. I'd ask Dodson, but I don't trust him."

"I agree," Sherri said.

But it was Dodson they confronted when they entered the study on the second floor.

The front door had been standing open, so they had hurried upstairs to the area where the light had shone from a window. As they had suspected, the room was the study.

The soft carpeting had muffled their footsteps and Dodson was taken completely by surprise.

Obviously unaware of their presence, he was sitting behind the big desk, searching intently through the papers he had piled high in front of him.

"I don't know what you're doing here," Josh said sternly, "but I would suggest you explain yourself!"

"Why, uh, ah," Dodson blustered. "Oh, it's you, again. Well, not that it's any of your concern, but I just got word that Fairbanks is dead according to some hospital in New York. I'm getting his affairs in order."

Spreading the fingers of his stubby hands on top of the piles of papers, Dodson's eyes narrowed. "Just what business do you think this is of yours, anyway?"

"As Joshua Fairbanks' grandson, it's very much my business."

"Well, I, uh . . ." Dodson looked as though he felt trapped, but his expression quickly shifted. "Why should I believe you're Fairbanks' heir?"

"I didn't say I'm his heir; I said I'm his grandson." Sherri could sense anger and frustration mounting in Josh's voice as he continued. "If you demand proof, or if there's any reason you're entitled to it, I'll be glad to come by your office tomorrow and discuss this matter."

After an extended silence, a look of shrewdness stole

over Dodson's face, and he stood as though in deference, rubbing his hands together slowly, "Well, now," he said in a conciliatory tone, "if you are a family member, I'm sure I can be of great help to you. Take all the details off your hands, so to speak."

Josh hesitated, not wanting to show his anger at this man's blatant trespassing. "Thank you. If I need your assistance, I'll get in touch with you. Now I suggest you leave."

Dodson got himself out of the room with as much poise as he could muster, leaving with a murmured repeat of his offer of help.

"That man," Sherri said. "What nerve!"

She had scarcely uttered the words when Dodson reappeared in the doorway. This time he completely ignored Josh and spoke directly to Sherri. "Ah, Miss McElroy, may I speak to you in private, please? Here in the hall, perhaps?"

Seeing her hesitation and her questioning glance to Josh, he said, "I'm sorry, of course, to bother you when you are busy."

Although Dodson disturbed her and she didn't want to be anywhere near him, Josh's imperceptible nod caused her to reconsider the refusal she was about to give.

Without a smile, she walked across the space between them and stepped past him into the hall.

He started to close the door behind them, but she reached over and shoved it open. Standing where she knew Josh could watch them, she turned to face Frank Dodson.

"Yes?" she asked, her icy demeanor revealing her distrust of him.

As he reached out to put his hand on her arm, Sherri, her lips tight, drew herself up primly with a small shudder.

Dodson's arm dropped swiftly to his side as though he'd had no such idea. "Ah, about our dinner date, Miss

McElroy, may I make reservations for, say, Thursday evening?"

"Dinner date?" Sherri had to swallow quickly in order to keep from giggling. Controlling herself, she said as seriously as possible, "Your offer is very flattering, Mr. Dodson, but as I've told you, my time here is taken up with other plans. Now if you'll excuse me."

Sherri stepped quickly back into the room before Dodson seemed to realize he'd been refused again. He was obviously flustered when the truth sank in. Then starting to follow her into the room, he said in a stage whisper, "But you don't understand. This could be mutually beneficial. I would see that you—" But Sherri was slowly but firmly shutting the door, forcing him to back out.

She closed the door firmly. "That man!" she said as Josh came toward her. "I believe he thinks I know something about your grandfather's business. He wanted to question me; I'm sure of it!"

———

When they returned to the car, Arnie said, "It was Dodson."

"So we discovered," Josh said. "He was going through papers in my grandfather's desk."

Arnie opened the door and got out as they were getting in. "I think I'd better try to talk to my dad. Tell Mrs. Kirk I appreciated the supper invitation, but I'll decline this time."

———

Sherri and Mrs. Kirk had cleared the table and were preparing to serve the dessert when the phone rang.

"I'll get it," Josh said.

When he had hung up, he seemed puzzled. "It was Arnie. He wants us to meet him at the station. His car is still here so he's using his dad's. He said there's something urgent he needs to discuss."

"He is most welcome to come here to the house, Josh," Mrs. Kirk said. "Would you like to call him back?"

"No, thanks, Martha. I'm sure he's already on his way."

"Well, then, you have him come over afterward for dessert. I have plenty extra," she smiled.

Josh asked Sherri to go along since Arnie had asked to see them both. "He sounded upset," Josh told her as they headed out the door.

Arnie arrived at the station just a minute after they had walked in and switched on the light over the old marred desk in a corner.

"You two alone?" he asked.

"Yes," Josh answered. "Why? What's up?"

Arnie dropped into one of the straight-backed chairs near a stack of tires while Sherri seated herself in the rocker. Josh sat in the desk's creaking swivel chair and turned to face Arnie.

"I hardly know what to tell you first," Arnie said, rubbing his forehead.

Then he looked up and began, "After I left you at the car, I walked home, going by the back way. Although it was almost dark and Dad hadn't put any lights on yet, I could just barely see him in the front room with someone. He switched on a light then, and I could see it was that lawyer, Dodson.

"As I got closer to the house," Arnie continued, "I could hear them clearly; they were both talking loudly. I heard Dad say, 'Look, I did that diggin' for you and I'm willin' to watch out for information for you, but I still ain't seen any of the cash you promised.' "

Arnie shook his head, worry clouding his face, "I don't know what Dad's got himself into. He's always seemed to be an honest man."

Josh reached over to touch Arnie's shoulder reassuringly. "Men do unexpected things sometimes for money."

Arnie nodded. "Dodson got real angry then, shaking his fist and shouting something about them both being more wealthy than they had ever dreamed, and that Dad could ruin it all. Then he stomped out and drove away."

His shoulders drooping, Arnie continued, "I waited a few minutes before I went in. Dad was just sitting there, staring straight ahead. I told him I'd overheard Dodson and asked if I could help him in some way. I wished then that we'd found it easier over the years to talk together."

Arnie shook his head slowly again, as though he were having trouble comprehending what had happened.

"What did he say?" Sherri asked.

"He seemed relieved to talk about it. He said Dodson was convinced that you and Josh are trying to steal something very valuable. And Dodson seems to think he's in some way entitled to it if he can find it."

"Did he say what he's looking for?" Josh asked.

"No, but he said he would pay Dad for watching you and any other trespassers on the property. He gave him the binoculars to use, and the gun to warn anyone away. It just does not make any sense to me. But he keeps trying to impress Dad with the fact that he'll be very rich if he cooperates."

"And now your dad's having second thoughts?" Josh asked.

"Yes. He said Dodson's been acting crazy lately, gets violent easily if he thinks Dad is backing out on their deal. Even threatened that Dad could go to prison for life if the truth were known."

"Does your dad know what Dodson is talking about?"

"He says he doesn't."

"Then try not to worry, Arnie," Josh said, reaching out to grasp Arnie's shoulder. "I promise to pray for your father and for you, too. God can resolve this situation, even though we feel helpless."

Giving Arnie a smile, Sherri said, "Martha has some pie waiting for us, Arnie. How about it?"

"Sounds great to me."

Mrs. Kirk joined them at the kitchen table, sitting with her knitting needles clicking softly. "What a good idea," Sherri said, going to get the coverlet she was working on.

When she returned, Arnie was asking, "Are we going again tomorrow?"

"I'm afraid I've strained Martha's good graces already," Josh returned.

"Now, Josh," Mrs. Kirk said, "I knew when I hired you that you might be here only a short while, and since no work is waiting in the garage, a few days away isn't going to put any hardship on me. Besides, your company and Sherri's more than repays me for any time off you take."

"Thanks, Martha," he smiled at her. He ate a bite of pie, then said, "I didn't tell you this earlier, knowing you would worry, but we were exploring a cave today."

"A cave? Around here?"

"Yes, it's on my grandfather's land, and it's immense."

"Well, I declare. I never heard of any caves in our area."

"Possibly no one else around here has either. It surprised us, too. Anyway, since you can see that we're back safely, I can tell you now that is where we are going tomorrow."

Noticing that she was looking concerned anyway, Josh added, "There's no reason to fear something may happen to us; we won't take any chances. Arnie is experienced at this and so am I. We'll plan to be back before dark. How's that?"

"All right," Mrs. Kirk sighed. "I'm sure I can trust you to be sensible and not take any foolish chances, but do be very, very careful."

Later, as Arnie left for home, Josh told him to meet them at the Fairbanks' front entrance at seven the next morning.

———————

Sherri and Josh arrived there at 6:30 and went directly to the study. He had asked her to put the key that opened the bookcase around her neck as she had worn it before.

"I'm going to need it this morning," he'd said, "and that's the safest place for it for now, so we don't lose it."

"We're going into the cave through the study opening?"

"Yes," Josh answered. "We'll open it ahead of time so Arnie will know only that there's an entrance in the building. I think I can trust him, but I feel a secret like that is best kept within the family."

"But, Josh," Sherri said, "then the secret is already ruined for you. I know about the desk and key, and I'm not in your family."

Sherri saw his eyes soften as he turned to her. "Who knows? Maybe we can change that," he said quietly. Josh stepped forward and put his arms around her, holding her very gently. "I realize we're just beginning to know each other," he continued with his face resting against her hair, "but in the past few days you've become so special to me."

Tipping her chin with his finger, he added, "And I know I want to know you more . . . much more." He kissed her gently on the forehead. Then dropping his arms, he picked up the key and chain she had placed on the desk when they came in.

Sherri stood a few moments where he'd left her, her thoughts whirling, while Josh opened the secret passage.

They met Arnie downstairs at the front door. "Sherri," Josh said, "I'm going to drive the car around to the side entrance where it won't be so noticeable. While I'm doing that, would you get a towel from the kitchen for me?"

She returned to the foyer with the towel just as Arnie and Josh came back in.

"Arnie," Josh said, "what I'm going to ask of you may seem ridiculous, but bear with me."

Refolding the towel into a long strip, he added, "Will you let me blindfold you? You'll understand why shortly."

Arnie looked at them quizzically. "What's this, a game? Sure, go ahead," he grinned, removing his helmet. "I'm sure your reason is a good one. Shall I leave my ropes and hat here for later?"

"No, hang on to them," Josh said, securing the blindfold.

"And hang on to me, too. Here, I'll take your helmet and rope."

"I'll walk on the other side of you, Arnie," Sherri said, taking his hand.

They moved fairly quickly across the foyer, up the stairs, and down the hall into the study.

Josh nodded to Sherri, and with Arnie's flashlight, she preceded them through the opening behind the bookcase. Josh carefully pulled it partway closed behind them.

Sherri led Arnie down the narrow stairs and through the first section of tunnel while Josh followed behind with the equipment.

After turning into the corridor leading off to the right, Josh said quietly to Sherri, "The other direction leads to your shaft and the area below. You probably missed this turn in the dark because you were walking along the opposite wall."

He stopped and said, "Arnie, you can remove the blindfold now."

Arnie stood with the towel in his hand, gazing around dumbfoundedly. "You mean we got here directly from the Fairbanks' house?"

"Right you are," Josh said. "For now, I didn't want to reveal the route."

"I don't blame you," Arnie said, still seeming somewhat bewildered. After adjusting the chin strap on the helmet he'd taken from Josh, he took his ropes.

"Oh, I just remembered. I stopped on the way home last night and got a roll of fluorescent tape," he said, taking it from a pocket and handing it to Josh.

Josh tore off a strip, walked back to the corner they had just turned, and stuck the tape about waist high on the wall. Then he removed the chalk mark he had put there. As he turned back, his light picked out a hand-sized stone lying at the base of the wall. Silently he picked it up and handed it to Sherri.

She drew in her breath. In dark, smudged letters was written "Job," with three distinct dots below it.

"The three dots I noticed yesterday, Josh. They're connected to the verses in Job. Remember in your letter it said there would be a map on the trip? Do you think those three dots we've been seeing are the map?"

"I'm sure of it," Josh nodded to her as she handed him the rock.

Arnie gave both of them a puzzled look. "A map to what? What are you two talking about?"

"I think it's time you know what we're doing in this cave," Josh said, turning to face Arnie. "Sherri found a letter from my grandfather that said he'd hidden something for me in here, though he didn't make clear just what it was, except that to him, it was a treasure. We came in here to look for it."

Arnie gave a half-whistle. "So we're treasure hunting? For a gas station mechanic, you're sure full of surprises!"

Josh laughed with him. "I'm sorry I didn't tell you before. I knew we needed your help to explore the cave, but I'm still not sure what this treasure is we're looking for. I didn't want to involve you too deeply in a situation I wasn't sure about."

"That's all right," Arnie reassured him. "I'm just glad I'm in on the excitement. Now, did you say these three-dot symbols will lead us to the treasure?"

"It's a guess," Josh replied, "but we won't know until we follow them and see."

"Well, let's get on with it," Sherri broke in, giving Josh a playful push. "We've got a treasure to find."

The corridor they had entered seemed to go deeper and deeper and led through several large rooms embellished with glorious rock formations.

Each time they went through an area with more than one opening or with parallel passages, Josh marked their way with strips of tape.

As they ducked to enter another narrower passage, Sherri heard the murmur of water, which grew louder as they moved along.

They turned a sharp corner and, after a short, damp passageway, Josh stepped out onto the shelf where they had been the previous day.

As she followed him, Sherri saw leaning against the wall on the ledge just to the left a flat rock with the now familiar three circles. She pointed excitedly to it; Josh nodded.

Checking through the last area of redwood-like columns they had been in the previous day, they discovered a small opening, marked with three circles, behind a pile of breakdown, almost covered by the debris. Crawling through, they found themselves in a cavern the size of an immense athletic dome. All three stood silently, gazing in awe.

Three of its sides sloped upward in bulges, curves and swirls to a roof high above. The fourth side of the cavern opened to a ledge which dropped off into a vast darkness.

Arnie beamed his powerful spotlight into the area below.

"It looks like a free-fall, Arnie," Josh said, "probably several hundred feet, or so. Should we try it?"

"Sure," Arnie answered as Sherri stepped back with a shudder.

Josh turned to her. "I noticed a small grotto over there where the upper slope meets this ledge. Let's see if it would be a safe place for you to wait for us."

Then he hesitated, continuing as though in apology, "Do you mind our leaving you here? It could be dangerous for you to come this time."

"Mind? Believe me, I have no desire to accompany you into that hole, none whatsoever," she assured him, laughing. "I just hope what we're looking for is waiting at the bottom."

"Thanks, Sherri," Josh said. "I'll leave my smaller flashlight, but under no circumstances should you leave this area." Looking beyond where they stood to the cavern's darkness, Sherri knew she would have no such desire.

The grotto proved to be a smoothly formed space about six feet high and six feet long, somewhat like the windowseat in her grandparents' bay window where Sherri snuggled as a child.

"Looks real cozy in there," Josh said, putting an arm easily around her shoulder. Then more earnestly, he said, "Sherri, it looks like Arnie and I will have a simple descent. We should be able to rappell it easily."

"Rappell?"

"Yes, go down on a rope. We'll want to scout around down there for clues and will plan to be back as soon as we can."

She lay her head against his shoulder for a moment. "I don't want any harm to come to you, Josh, so I can't help worrying a little."

He held her for a moment, then released her and turned

to walk toward Arnie, who was stooping near the rim of the ledge.

She watched the two as they worked with their ropes, fastening them to a couple of the larger stalagmites near the edge of the abyss. Their lights glinted on metal devices they were utilizing.

Then Josh waved to her and disappeared over the rim. A moment later, Arnie followed.

Without the glow of their lights, the darkness was intense and more frightening. Sherri was glad Josh had found the little grotto for her. Once inside, the light from her helmet created a warm glow. Sherri leaned back against the hard rock. This whole adventure was going to make some tale for Mrs. Kirk!

She smiled at the thought of the warm, caring woman, remembering their conversation of two nights ago. The woman had suffered so much, yet she had peace; joy, even, when she had every right to be bitter and angry. *How I envy her peace,* Sherri thought with a sigh.

Then Mrs. Kirk's words came back to her. "You can experience His love, Sherri. He wants to be kind to you, but He can't while you are pushing Him away."

"Pushing Him away." She rolled the words over in her mind. Was that what she had been doing? After her parents' deaths, had He been there all the time, longing to comfort and help her while she'd refused?

Then she began to recount the help she had experienced. The people who stayed so close to her when she got the news of the accident. Her grandparents' insistence on doing all they could to be a real family to her, even as they faced their own grief. The way it had worked out at the last minute for her to transfer to a nursing school near them.

Sherri began to cry softly. "Oh, Lord," she wept, "you were always with me, providing all these things. I was never alone, but I didn't feel your love because I refused to." She breathed deeply for a moment.

"I'm so sorry for the anger and bitterness I've felt toward you. I've been angry because life didn't go my way. Please forgive me. From now on, let my life go *your* way, and make me what you want me to be."

She rested her face in her hands, and sat quietly, sinking into the relaxation that comes when a struggle is over. Peace like she had never known flowed into her, filling her heart.

Raising her head and looking up into the darkness, she said, "Thank you, Lord, for cleansing me. I feel so new. And I sense your presence with me here."

I can't wait to tell Josh, she thought, smiling at the joy she knew he'd feel for her. She rose and walked a few paces toward the ledge, then stopped to listen. No sign of Josh and Arnie yet. She sat down again, and removing her helmet, placed it on the floor beside her.

As she did, the beam from its light shot straight across the grotto into the area below a scalloped shelf-like protrusion. The sparkle was dazzling.

Curious, she put the helmet back on, picked up the flashlight, and headed across to the opposite wall.

Below the shelf, on the floor close to the wall, were three smudged dots, and right above them, in the wall halfway between the floor and the shelf, was a horizontal slit, approximately one foot by two feet.

Getting down on her knees and elbows, Sherri shined the light into the opening.

Brilliant sparkles struck from every surface of a tiny cubicle, like the inside of a crystal ball.

In the very center of the sphere-like room rose a speleothem, sparkling like snow!

"I've found it!" Sherri cried. "Josh's legacy, the treasure of the snow!"

15

The time before Josh and Arnie returned seemed like an eternity to Sherri. She was tempted to try entering the crystal nook, but remembering how her last attempt at exploring a cave alone had ended, decided against it.

Finally she heard voices coming from beyond the ledge, and before long a glow of ever-widening brightness appeared above the rim as one of them made his way up over the edge.

"You okay, Sherri?" It was Josh's voice.

"Yes," she called, going toward him. "Oh, Josh! I believe I've found the hiding place of your treasure-of-the-snow. There's a slit in the wall of the grotto, and it leads into a small, beautiful area. When you see it, you'll understand."

Arnie appeared at the edge of the ledge just then, so Sherri excitedly repeated her news to him. She barely allowed the men time to remove their equipment before she pulled them both toward the grotto.

Josh dropped to his knees and guided a beam of light under the shelf, then gave a low whistle. "You may be right, Sherri," he said excitedly.

Feeling carefully around the perimeter of the oblong opening, he located several sections at its bottom that moved beneath his probing grip.

"They are wedged together perfectly," he said in amazement, "just like bricks around a window."

After he had pulled them out, shifting them carefully to

161

the floor, the opening doubled in its vertical size.

Pushing his flashlight in ahead of him, Josh wriggled through. "It's completely dry in here," he called to Arnie and Sherri crouching together at the opening.

"Hey, hang on!" Arnie yelled back to him. "I'll come in and help you look. My flashlight is more powerful than yours." Arnie reached toward his belt for the large flash.

"It's gone," he said disgustedly. "I had it when we came in here, though. I must have dropped it when I was on the other side of the cavern checking out those passages." He pushed himself upright and headed to the far end of the large room. The glow of his headlamp disappeared as he moved behind the cluster of rocks to search for his light.

Just then Josh gave a shout, and Sherri leaned into the opening, straining to see. "Josh, what is it?"

Josh had turned, and was moving quickly toward the opening. "It's a treasure, Sherri," he panted hard as he pulled himself through the opening. "Gold bars. Lots of them. Stacked behind the pile of crystal you thought looked like snow."

Sherri threw her arms around him and squealed her delight. "We did it! After this, you're about to get all you deserve!"

"You're right about that, missy," a harsh voice rumbled behind her. Sherri whirled to find herself staring into the evil, twisted face of Frank Dodson.

"And I'm going to claim what's mine," he growled, stepping close enough so they could see the hard, shiny steel of the revolver he was pointing at them.

Sherri gasped and froze in terror. Josh stepped in close behind her, his hands tight on her shoulders. "What do you want, Dodson?" he demanded.

"Why, the same thing you want," Dodson sneered. "The money, of course. Fairbanks' treasure."

Josh tried to sound casual, covering his fear. "What

makes you think there's a treasure?"

"Don't play games with me," Dodson snorted. "I've known for a long time Fairbanks had money hidden somewhere in the house. Why do you think I became his attorney and worked so hard to gain his confidence? All I didn't know was where to find it."

He took a step closer, brandishing the revolver. "When Fairbanks told me he had a grandson, I started to get worried. Then when the hospital in New York notified me the old coot was dead, I knew I was going to have to find the money before this grandson of his showed up and claimed the house."

He took another step toward them. "Now with you out of the way, Stevens, there's no heir, and I've got the treasure, too." He laughed, a high-pitched evil laugh.

Sherri's face was ashen, and her breath came in short, broken pants. Josh moved now to her side, partly shielding her from Dodson. Her trembling fingers clenched his arm. Even in the dim light, she was sure Dodson could see her fear.

"I couldn't have done it without your help, though," Dodson said, mocking them. "Oh, I found the letter in Fairbanks' desk, so I had the treasure map he'd drawn, but it never made sense. I never thought about the trail being *underground*—not until today. If you hadn't left that bookcase ajar, and your trail so well-marked, I never would have found you."

Dodson flashed his light around the high rock wall behind them, then took a few steps toward the edge of the chasm, scanning the area with his beam. Then he turned back toward them. "The treasure," he growled, his voice raspy, "where is it?"

Josh said nothing, and Sherri could feel his body tense and see his fists clench. "Come on. Where is it?" Dodson persisted. "Let's not have any heroics here," he warned Josh menacingly. "I'd just as soon shoot you now as later. You won't be the first I've killed for this money."

Sherri stared at him, the meaning of what he'd just said slowly sinking in. Her voice shook as she spoke. "The woman I saw in the study . . . the dead woman . . . you killed her? Why?"

"It was her own fault," Dodson whined. "She was a cleaning woman or something. She caught me in the study the day I found Fairbanks' letter with the map. Had to know what I was doing there. Had to stick her nose in. When she threatened to call the police, I shot her."

Then he glared at Sherri, his face twisted with hate and greed. "I thought somebody would see me if I took her body out then, so I figured I'd come back after dark for her. Would have worked just fine, too, but you, you messed up everything!"

"It was your car I heard leaving the mansion that night," Sherri gasped, her voice barely audible.

"It was me, all right," he said. "Thought I had my problem solved, too. When I saw your car, I figured I'd found someone to take the rap for the old woman's murder. That's why I messed up your engine. Figured then you'd be stranded, so I'd have time to call the police and report an intruder in the mansion. They'd find you and the body, and I'd get off scot-free."

"But no police came that night," Josh broke in, trying to divert Dodson's attention away from Sherri.

"Of course they didn't," Dodson grunted at him with disgust. "When I went to use Morrow's phone, he told me the girl was a friend of Fairbanks, so I knew the intruder story wouldn't work. So, I came back up the side road and sneaked in and dragged the body out without anybody ever knowing about it."

Sherri reached out for the wall behind her to steady herself as she felt her knees weaken. Dodson knew he had the upper hand now, and was relishing every moment of their panic. He made a step toward her, and Sherri screamed as he let his light fall and grabbed her wrist, roughly twisting her arm, pulling her away from Josh. "Killing that old woman didn't bother me, and killing her won't either. So the money," he glared at Josh, "where is it?"

Sherri felt the hard steel barrel pressed into her side as Dodson stepped closer to the edge of the pit, jerking her along with him.

Suddenly the powerful beam of Arnie Morrow's flashlight cut through the darkness directly into Dodson's eyes, blinding him. Dodson gave a cry and stumbled back.

Sherri grabbed frantically at the tall stalagmite beside her as Dodson swayed backward, his grip on her wrist loosening. Then strong hands grabbed her waist, pulling her forward and away from the chasm.

A sickening horror overwhelmed Sherri as, held tight in Josh's arms, she covered her ears to shut out the hideous sound of Dodson's horrible shriek as he hurtled downward over the brink of the chasm and into the darkness.

16

With one arm still holding her close, Josh led Sherri across the wide expanse of rock floor through the giant cavern of stalagmite landscape, back to the place where they had entered the gigantic dome earlier that day. That morning seemed years away to Sherri as she walked numbly along.

Arnie followed silently behind, carrying his and Josh's equipment.

It wasn't until they reached the little slow-moving stream with the rimstone pool and stopped to rest that Sherri realized how far they had come.

Although Josh's nearness was reassuring, the horror of what had happened was heavy on her mind. She felt close to falling apart.

————

When they got back to Mrs. Kirk's, Josh helped Sherri from the car to the porch. Mrs. Kirk rose and smiled as they came in, but her smile faded into concern as she saw Sherri's drained face and disheveled appearance.

"Martha," Josh said, "Sherri needs to lie down while I make some phone calls. She's all right, but she's had an unexpectedly rough day."

"Of course," she said. The older woman took Sherri's arm and helped her to the bedroom.

After she pulled a quilt over Sherri, Mrs. Kirk gently

brushed the girl's hair back from her forehead. "You three seem so silent, and I've never seen Josh look so stern. Are you sure you're all right? Did something happen? Is there something you want to tell me?"

Sherri nodded and started to cry softly. "It was awful, Mrs. Kirk, just terrible," and she wept for a moment as Mrs. Kirk patted her. "Please, I think you'd better have Josh tell you."

"Of course, dear. You just try to rest now."

————

It was dark when Sherri woke. Switching on the lamp, she stared unbelieving at her watch; she had slept almost six hours. From the other parts of the house, she could hear the murmur of voices.

She slipped into a fresh pair of jeans and a sweater and went to join the others.

When she entered the kitchen, she found Mrs. Kirk carrying coffee to the table where a slim, tired-looking woman in a pink housedress sat next to Ross Morrow.

Sherri started when she saw him, but Arnie stepped forward, reassuring her. "Mom, this is Sherri McElroy," he said, taking Sherri's arm and leading her to the group at the table. "You've already met my dad, Sherri."

Gaining her composure, and remembering the events of the afternoon, Sherri searched Arnie's face, then Josh's. Did these people know about Dodson? How much should she say?

"You've been with your sister, Mrs. Morrow," Sherri turned to her. "Is she feeling better?"

Mrs. Morrow's red-rimmed eyes made it apparent that she had been weeping. "She passed away the morning after I arrived. I stayed for the funeral and just returned this afternoon."

"It's okay, Sherri," Josh broke in, moving to pull up a

chair beside her at the table. "The Morrows know all about Dodson. Mrs. Kirk does, too. While you were asleep we called the police and a cave rescue team to bring his body up."

Ross Morrow shook his head as he looked down into his coffee cup. "Who'd have thought Dodson was the one tryin' to steal Mr. Fairbanks' money? He had me convinced it was you two who was the guilty ones. And to think he up and killed Mrs. Clemons!"

Sherri asked softly, "Was that her name, Mrs. Clemons?"

"Yes," Mrs. Morrow said sadly, tears brimming in her eyes. "She was a widow, fairly new in town, with no relatives at all."

Mrs. Morrow paused, dabbing at her eyes with a handkerchief she had taken from her dress pocket. "We'd become acquainted over the past few months, and I knew she wanted extra work. So when I had to go to be with my sister, I asked her to take over my duties at Mr. Fairbanks' house. We had gotten a message that you were coming, Miss McElroy, so I wanted things all ready."

Mrs. Morrow sniffed and took a small gulp of coffee.

"While I was at my sister's, I thought I'd give Mrs. Clemons a call, to be sure she was doin' all right, but there was no answer. I tried the mansion and her house several times. It didn't make sense to me and I got worried."

The graying lady let out a deep sigh. "She was a responsible one, Mrs. Clemons. Hard workin', too. I knew she wouldn't have just up and left without tellin' no one. That's when I called you, son."

Arnie reached across the table and patted her hand to comfort her as she continued. "I thought something must be wrong, and I knew you was coming, Miss McElroy, so I told Arnie to warn you there might be danger."

She looked down, then at the faces around the table. "I

didn't say more because I didn't know for sure what was wrong. Didn't want no one thinkin' I was a silly old woman, imagining things."

Josh rose from the table and brought the coffeepot from the stove. "The only piece to this puzzle still missing," he said, refilling the older woman's cup, "is what Dodson did with her body. If we could find it, the police could match the gunshot wound to Dodson's gun, and his guilt would be unquestioned."

As he spoke, Morrow twisted nervously in his chair, his face beginning to glisten with perspiration beneath the kitchen's overhead light.

Then he spoke reluctantly. "Think I may know where her body is. Over in the field next to the pasture. Dodson, he had me dig a big hole there the night of the storm. Promised to pay me a lot to do it *that* night. Said his dog had died and he didn't have any place to bury it. How could I have been so dumb?"

Morrow's shoulders drooped even lower than they had been, and he shook his head slowly. "I noticed he was actin' nervous and funny, and he was drivin' in the dark and rain without the car lights on. I asked him if he was havin' trouble with them, but he said no. Told me to mind my own business.

"I asked him should I help carry the dog to the hole and he said he could do it, that I should go on home. I sure thought it was funny, buryin' a dog way out here when there musta been plenty spots closer to town. Guess the promise of the money clouded my thinking, and I just pushed them questions right out of my mind."

Then Morrow looked up at Josh, a startled look on his face. "Do you suppose they'll think I had somethin' to do with her killing? I didn't, honest. I didn't know anything about it until tonight."

"Try not to worry. We'll tell the police about it in the

morning," Josh answered, putting his hand encouragingly on Morrow's shoulder.

———

Later when everyone else had departed and Mrs. Kirk had retired, Josh asked, "Would you like to take a stroll?"

With a soft smile, Sherri nodded.

Josh opened the door and they stepped out onto the front porch. It was an unusually warm night and the fragrance of the flowers along the walk wafted up to them.

"Josh, tonight you didn't mention the gold in the cave. Did you get it out?"

"Not yet," Josh said, taking her hand and drawing it up inside the crook of his arm as they walked. "It's safe, though. The cave is sealed off now. Arnie and I will get it tomorrow.

"Now, Sherri, let's put all the bad things out of our minds and enjoy being together. We need to thank God that you are safe, that Dodson didn't pull you over the rim with him."

Sherri smiled up at him. "You're right, Josh. We have so much to thank Him for! Do you mind if I do it right now?"

Josh looked at her, surprised and pleased. "Sure. I'd appreciate that."

They both closed their eyes as Sherri prayed, "Oh, Lord, you've been so kind to us. Thank you for keeping us safe." Then she paused a moment. "Thank you, too, for the new awareness of your love I've discovered in this place. I don't know what you have for our futures, but I want to trust you and follow your leading."

As she breathed a soft "Amen" and looked up, Josh put his free hand over hers and gave it a squeeze.

Except for the occasional call of a nighthawk swooping through the darkness, there was silence as they walked slowly along the flagstones.

They were nearing a curve adjacent to the pond when Josh's steps slowed, then stopped. Raising his hands to Sherri's shoulders and turning her toward him, he tenderly touched her chin and tilted her head back to receive his gentle kiss.

Then he put his arms around her and Sherri snuggled happily against him.

"You're quite a lady, Sherri McElroy," he said softly, "and I think I may be falling in love with you."

After a few moments he released her, and taking her hand, started back toward the house. As they left the pond, Sherri saw the reflection of the stars on the water's smooth surface, and wondered if they matched the ones she felt must be evident in her eyes.

17

The rest of the week passed swiftly for Sherri.

After Mrs. Clemons was unearthed from her shallow grave and the police had satisfied themselves about Dodson's death, serenity finally descended on Mrs. Kirk's little home.

On Friday afternoon, Josh checked over the Mustang, and Sherri had the gas tank filled at the Kirk station. That night Martha prepared a farewell supper, and Sherri left for her grandparents' home the next morning just as the sun was rising.

Josh phoned her Saturday night. "Sherri, can't you come back here, at least for a while? We have so many things to discuss concerning the future."

"Oh, Josh, I wish I could. But I've promised Gram I'd be with them two weeks. Then I must get back to New York. I have a new job waiting at St. James Hospital."

"Okay, Sherri, I understand. But, do I miss you! Try to arrange for some time off soon, will you, because I can't get away right now, either. I'll be tied up with Grandfather's affairs for a while."

"Yes, Josh, I will. I miss you, too."

Then just before she replaced the receiver, she heard him whisper, "Don't forget, I love you."

———

Every day during her stay at her Grandparents'

brought either a phone call or a letter from Josh.

His expressions of caring followed her to New York and continued through the months of work at the hospital. The extended time of phone conversations and correspondence brought a closeness and understanding that even proximity may not have afforded.

Both of them lived for the Fourth of July vacation, when Sherri could come to Scarborough for a few days. But late in June, one of the nurses on her floor was injured in an auto accident and another was forced to take an early emergency maternity leave.

Reluctantly, Sherri phoned Josh. "I feel I really should stay and help out, Josh," she said, sensing his disappointment.

"You're right, honey," Josh said, "but I can't wait any longer to see you. If I fly in early Sunday morning, can you spend the day with me?"

Sherri drew in her breath, a gasp of joy, "Yes, Josh! Oh, yes!"

———

Sunday dawned very warm and bright, promising a beautiful day.

Sherri had a breakfast of orange juice, warm sweet rolls, and coffee ready at the cozy table in her apartment kitchen when Josh arrived.

Sherri flung open the door, and as he stood there, tall and handsome, her heart overflowed with love, and she threw her arms around him.

Neither of them spoke. Josh held her tightly for several minutes. Then Sherri lifted her face; the gentleness of his lips against hers was soft, questioning. She leaned against him, her arms slipping around his neck.

Then he lifted his head, and as she laid hers against his

chest, she heard the double-time thudding of his heart in her ear.

"I love you, Sherri," he said, his voice filled with emotion as he rested his cheek against her hair. "I never imagined love could happen so quickly, or that it could be so strong, so sure, in such a short time."

Gazing into her face, he added softly, "Sherri, I know it's very soon to ask, and I'll wait for an answer as long as you like until you can be sure, but will you . . . do you care enough about me to be my wife?"

"Yes, Josh," she whispered. "I'll marry you. I love you more than I can say."

"Thank you," he said, stroking her hair. A short, joyful laugh escaped his lips as he again pressed his lips to hers.

Their day together sped by. Following an early service at the old cathedral within walking distance of Sherri's apartment building, they had lunch at one of her favorite restaurants, then spent the afternoon walking in the park.

At dusk, he kissed her goodbye outside her apartment door, scarcely hearing the cab driver honking impatiently to remind him he might miss his plane.

"Thanksgiving in Scarborough, Sherri, not one day later. That's a promise?"

"Yes, Josh, that's a promise."

———

Thanksgiving at Martha Kirk's was a holiday without equal. Besides Sherri and Josh, Martha had invited Sherri's grandparents to join them, so her little house buzzed with laughter and warmth and the wonderful aroma of baking. And to complete the joy of the celebration, Sherri proudly showed off the sparkling diamond engagement ring Josh had chosen for her.

During the sumptuous holiday dinner around Martha's

large kitchen table, Josh and Sherri shared with the others their plans for the future.

"We'll be married in Scarborough at Christmastime, God willing," Josh said, "and next year I'll enter medical school at Indiana University."

Buttering a roll, he continued, smiling at Sherri, "We want to turn the mansion into a farm-home-counseling center for troubled teenagers. Martha, we hope you'll make your home there with us as a resident-grandmother; Mr. and Mrs. Carborg, you're invited, too. You're all three most welcome—and needed."

"We're praying that we will be able to give those young people a pleasant, stable home," Sherri said, "and to help them understand how God can enable them to overcome their problems."

"Well, Josh," Mrs. Kirk said, looking fondly at both of them, "it seems as though God has given you a great opportunity to do exactly what He impressed on your heart some time ago—a real miracle, I'd say."

"Yes," Josh said gratefully, "and all the resources I'll need to accomplish the task."

Getting up and going to stand behind Sherri, he rested his hands on her shoulders. As she turned her head to look up at him, he said, "And to me, the greatest God-given treasure of all is right here, my wife-to-be—my beautiful Sherri."